# PROBAI

# PROBABLE FEAR

## By
## Julie Trettel

Probable Fear
Westin Force Delta: Book Three
Copyright ©2023, Julie Trettel. All rights reserved.
Cover Art by, Booking it Designs

## Thanks and Acknowledgments

Huge thanks to Jordan Truex for making this book happen. It's been a rough month. Without you I don't know what I would have done. Thanks for being my rock and my cheerleader ensuring this book actually made deadline. We did it!

# Colin

## Chapter 1

It should have been me. The fact that Linc had taken a bullet for me was eating me alive. It should have been me.

Sure, he was going to be fine, but that wasn't the point. We had each other's backs on the team and logically I knew if the roles had been reversed that I would not have hesitated to take a bullet for him. But Linc was newly mated. He had a lot to live for. It should have been me.

Combine that with the realization that it had happened at all, and I had landed myself in a very dark place I couldn't seem to crawl out of. This wasn't me. This wasn't the man I was and definitely not the one I wanted to be, but I didn't know how to dig out of the darkness threatening to overcome me.

There was no rhyme or reason for it. I was fine. Linc was fine. There was no permanent damage done on the outside, but inside, I was battling demons I didn't even know I had. It was enough that the others were starting to take notice too.

"I'm worried about him," I overheard Tucker tell Michael. "It's bad enough that after running into him at the grocery store, Annie even asked me if he was okay. And let's face it, my mate never notices anything that doesn't directly involve her. It's bad, and we've left him to suffer on his own for too long."

"I don't know what to do," Michael explained. "He's doing everything right, yet it's obvious he's not okay. Patrick is noticing and asking if we need to be concerned. He mentioned possibly replacing him. None of us want that."

"So order him to counseling. Isn't that why Lachlan was brought on to the team to begin with?"

"As a resource, sure. To help those rescued adjust to a free life again, absolutely. But I never really thought I'd have to force one of my guys to go talk to him."

"Well do it. It's better than just losing him. Colin's one of us and we need him on this team. You can't just replace him because he's suffering right now."

"I don't even understand what he's suffering with. I mean, is he sick? Is he hurt? He's just shut me out and won't talk about it."

"So make him. That's Lachie's job for crying out loud."

"Hey, what's up? And what do you need me to do?" Lachlan asked, and I groaned internally not wanting to alert them to my presence.

I dragged myself to work every single day. Sure, I wasn't entirely okay, but I was here. I worked harder than anyone and pushed myself to the brink of exhaustion just in hopes of sleeping at night. I knew things were bad. I wasn't an idiot. I just didn't know how to pull myself out of this funk I was in. Every time I tried, there was this little voice inside the back of my head telling me I was going to just get someone else hurt again or worse, killed.

It was stupid, but even knowing better couldn't stop the sense of doom hanging over me.

"How would you feel about scheduling some time with Colin?" Michael asked him.

"You know, like your head shrinking shit. Fix him," Tucker insisted.

Walker laughed. "I don't think that's quite how that works."

"Well, we have to do something." Tucker continued to persist.

"I feel like this is all my fault," Linc told them.

"It's no one's fault," Lachlan insisted. "That last big mission just screwed with his head."

"Tell me about it. He's brought over so many meals that Christine asked me to make him stop. The freezer is full. We'll be eating for months off of it, and while I appreciate it all, I'm sorry to say, he just isn't the best cook."

That made them all laugh as I cringed. I'd tried. Lord knew I tried, but I also knew he was right. I was not a good cook. Still, it was almost an obsession of mine to ensure that Linc and Christine had everything they could possibly need. I hadn't just cooked for them, but I regularly went shopping or showed up to fix things around their house. Maybe it was a little invasive, but I couldn't seem to stop myself.

"I've been back to work for six weeks now and I'm fine, but I think he still somehow feels guilty for me getting shot, when I'm the one that pushed him out of the way. It doesn't make sense."

"Linc, it's classic signs of survivor's guilt. I've tried to talk to him, but so far, he shuts me out or finds an excuse to walk away," Lachlan admitted.

"Which he couldn't do if he was directly ordered to be there," Tucker pointed out.

"I mean it would at least get him in my office for an extended time where he couldn't just run away."

"I don't like it, but I can't keep ignoring this," Michael agreed.

"We could try an intervention. Maybe get him to see he hasn't been acting like himself," Walker suggested.

I growled. "Don't you think I know that?" I blurted out, making them all jump as I rounded the corner to face them.

"You're here," Michael said. "Great."

Clearly, they hadn't heard my arrival. We were already ten minutes late for warmups, of course I was here.

"Let's get to work then. I'm tired of trying to lead these assholes in workouts every day. That's your job," Linc told me, acting as if nothing had just transpired through the team.

I cringed. I constantly felt like I was letting myself down, but I tried to overcompensate and do more, work harder, and push the others to do the same. Was it really that obvious? Was I somehow letting my team down, too? That was the last thing I wanted.

Holding my head high, I forced myself to act normal and ran a smooth but hard workout. The others all fell into line, and there was no more mention of their concerns about me.

I was still numb through it all and didn't even realize just how hard I was pushing them until Walker nearly collapsed and begged for a break.

As I looked around the room one thing was painfully clear. My attempts at normal had fallen short. I'd overcompensated again and they all knew it. I could see the concern evident in each of their eyes and it made me feel even lower.

"Let's take a break," I said, trying my best to sound cheerful even though it fell flat even to my own ears. "I think you assholes are getting soft on me." My attempt at humor also fell short.

There was an awkwardness I'd never felt before in the silence surrounding us. I sighed knowing it was because of me and hating myself for it.

Maybe they'd just be better off without me. I could talk to Kyle about stepping down from Delta. Perhaps he'd even let me continue working at Westin Force in another capacity. I could do paperwork or something, at least, without causing too much harm to anyone.

That's when my mind drifted off to all the ways I could screw that up too. I shivered. Man, papercuts were a bitch. What if an infection set in and killed someone?

As irrational as it was, I knew I was simply spiraling back into that dark place. In some ways it was comfortable there, like a familiar blanket that made me feel like without me around everyone I cared about would be fine, better off even.

That line of thought always terrified me the most.

I couldn't do this.

"Don't," Lachlan said quietly. "Just take a deep breath. You're doing great."

My jaw locked as I gritted my teeth and nodded.

"I can help you if you let me," he added. "You're going to be ordered to go through counseling anyway."

I hated the idea of pouring out my deepest fears to anyone, but especially to one of my Delta brothers.

"I'm fine. I don't need counseling," I said. "Break's over," I barked at the rest of them.

I knew I was pushing them too hard. I was moving beyond my fear to a complete numbness. I'd been here before. In some weird way, it was a step in the right direction, but also the hardest to dig myself back out of. I needed to feel something, anything aside from the emptiness that was threatening to break me again. Yet the fear of hurting someone else held me back and left me stranded in a battle of depression.

Some days I didn't even want to get out of bed, but I forced myself anyway. I had notes throughout my house reminding me that I had been saved for a reason. It wasn't enough to stop the depression, but just enough for me to guiltily drag my ass out of bed and show up every single day.

When Tucker collapsed and begged for a break, I didn't miss the looks of concern throughout the room. They weren't for him. They were for me.

Michael nodded to Lachlan and then pulled me aside.

"We need to talk."

I sighed. "I know what's coming. I already overhead everything."

"Okay then. So, schedule some sessions with Lachlan."

I gritted my teeth, hating that I'd let things snowball to this point. But I nodded.

The relief on Michael's face made me cringe.

Still, as the days proceeded, I avoided Lachlan as much as possible and I refused to schedule my first session. On the rare occasion that he cornered me, I'd come up with an excuse of why it wasn't a good time for me.

Instead, I kept my head down and did my job. I picked up extra shifts for perimeter runs. And I continued trying to help Linc and Christine, consumed by the guilt of letting him take that bullet for me.

Nearly a week had passed before Michael cornered me again.

"Stop putting this off, Colin. That's an order. Schedule a session with Lachlan or you're grounded until I figure out what to do with you."

# Mirage

## Chapter 2

"Good morning, my pets," the Collector said as he strolled through the corridor looking in on each of us.

I never knew their names, and he was far from my first.

Collectors. That's what we knew them as. They collected people like me. Witches. We weren't like witches on TV with magical potions and spells. We were just people with extra gifts. I had two extra gifts really, not that I would ever allow him to find that out.

My family came from a long line of wolf shifters. He had a fox shifter in captivity and thought that was his gift, shapeshifting. It wasn't really a gift though. I still remembered life in a Pack even though it was a lifetime ago. I knew the stories my mother had told me, and sometimes, I could feel my wolf just beneath the surface of my skin. She wanted out. She wanted to protect me. I was certain of this, but I never allowed it.

Some of my previous Collectors had known about shifters, and a few even seemed to think that all witches were shifters. Maybe they'd been right, but it wasn't something I was dumb enough to ask about.

For the most part I kept my head down and my mouth shut. It helped keep me alive and offered me a comfortable enough life.

I wasn't particularly fond of my latest Collector. I'd been traded to him just six months ago. He was nice enough, but paranoid when it came to his collection. It was why he had so desperately wanted me.

He was fanatical about security and each of us had been microchipped on arrival. Worse than that was the implant he'd added to the back of my neck. Everyone in his collection had one, but his switch to activate it wasn't set up to attack individually. Nope. With the switch of a button, he essentially tazed all of us at once. It was quite effective in ensuring our cooperation. And if someone didn't acquiesce, the lot of us would demand submission after a jolt or two.

Most of the Collectors took good care of us. We were special to them. But not all of them were good. I'd heard nightmarish tales from some of the witches and was thankful that so far, I'd been one of the luckier ones.

The first Collector came to acquire me at the age of eight. I tried to hold on to the memories I had of my family before then, but as the years passed, they faded. I could still recount the stories though. I knew my history, and I had learned the importance of hiding it.

Sometimes I wondered what it would be like to let my wolf out to stretch. I vividly remembered the magnificent beasts my mother and father would shift into. If I closed my eyes, I could still remember the feel of their soft fur and the smell of the wild on their skin even in human form.

"Good morning, Mirage," he said with a sly grin, jolting me from my memories.

"Good morning, sir."

Putting on a smile and staying friendly with the Collector was key to a healthy life.

"Would you be so kind as to transport me this morning. Pretty please? Just for a few minutes?"

I wanted to groan. I should have refused, but I'd learned a long time ago that being stubborn and refusing to use my gift only caused pain and harm, not just to me, but to everyone in the collection.

"Where would you like to go today, sir?"

The sweet tone of my voice sickened me, but it was a game I played for survival and if I was lucky and played my part right, then he would leave me be to live a quiet life inside my small suite.

My room consisted of a single bed, with a real mattress and nice linens. There was also a small loveseat and a television that only played one movie at a time on repeat. I also had a nice little bathroom all to myself. Compared to most places I'd lived, this was pretty nice and I liked it well enough here.

We weren't served food in our rooms. Instead, he let us out to eat in the small cafeteria. It was nice talking to the others and putting faces with voices. In my previous collections, I was lucky if I saw anyone aside from maybe the witch in the cell across the hall from me.

"How about Aruba?" he asked.

I nodded. "Certainly."

Concentrating on the pictures of the beach and sea I'd been shown on my arrival—along with other places he loved—I channeled that image. A shimmer radiated from me and soon it was as if he were alone on the beach in Aruba as he basked in the sun while swearing he could feel the cool water as the waves broke against the shore.

For me, I saw him as if through a veil. He wasn't even aware of my presence, but I was aware of him. It was just a mirage, a trick of the brain making him believe he was temporarily transported there. He saw what I wanted him to see.

That was how I'd landed my name: Mirage. If I had another before my powers set in, then it was long gone. I'd been called Mirage for as long as I could remember.

"Thank you, Mirage," he finally said as I pulled my power back inside me and his oasis faded away.

It seemed like a small insignificant thing to do for him. I really didn't mind much. So far he hadn't abused it, but I also hadn't gotten up the courage to say no to him. Since he had that implant put into place, I was terrified to even try.

One witch had angered him. I wasn't even sure why, but we'd all been punished for it. I swore I would do everything in my power to never feel that pain again.

I shivered.

"Are you cold, my dear?" he asked.

"Maybe a little," I confessed.

"Why don't you head on down to breakfast now?" he suggested as he unlocked my door.

"Okay."

I didn't make it a point to hang out with my owner any more than I had to. Using food as my excuse to leave, I quickly made my way to the cafeteria.

"Again?" Magnolia asked.

"Yup. It's becoming an everyday thing and he really wants to go to Aruba."

"Good. Let him."

"Shush, Mags. You can't talk like that."

"I'm just saying, if that's his desire, clearly he has the money for it, so he should go. What is so wrong with that?"

I cut my eyes in her direction just as she rolled hers.

Mags hadn't been in a collection before. This was all new to her, and her natural instinct was to rebel against it all and even try to escape. Maybe because I had been so young when I was first taken, I just didn't have that rebellion in me.

This was my life. It wasn't the best, but I couldn't imagine it was the worst either. Plus, it just wasn't in my nature to focus on the negatives or the things I couldn't control.

I had a gift. Other people could choose to exploit that gift. I'd certainly heard plenty of stories such as that, but I never really felt like that was happening to me. When push came to shove if I felt that my powers were being exploited, I would push back, but that had rarely occurred in my life. Who cared if this Collector wanted to pretend to lay out on a beach in Aruba?

At one time in my life, it would have worn me out and weakened me to make that happen for him, but at this point I'd done it so many times that it was like second nature. I didn't even bat an eye and knew I could sustain it for hours if I had to.

Breakfast included scrambled eggs, bacon, fruit, and toast. I filled my plate and then joined Mags, Gwen, and Ned at a table. The collection here was small. There were only eight of us in total. I'd never seen a collection so small before. My previous collections had been passed down from generation to generation. The largest probably had over five hundred, maybe more. I had never really left my cell there, but I'd heard the Collector bragging about it plenty of times.

For the most part, I liked it here. I had friends, and it felt more like a home than any other collection I'd ever lived in.

As I looked around, I smiled. Ramona had her head together plotting something or another with Cypress and Boris while Atlas sat alone brooding in the corner.

Growing up, I'd gotten to watch a lot of TV, or at least the stuff my Collector allowed. I wasn't a complete idiot. I listened to those around me recount stories of the real world, but I'd been on the inside for close to twenty years now. To me, this was the real world.

Still, I had never really understood why everyone on television was so happy all the time. They laughed a lot, and things were never really that serious. I'd managed to hold on to that image and tried to stay as positive as I believed them to be in the real world, but until I came here, it had been little more than just another mirage.

Boris said something I couldn't hear as Ramona and Cypress burst out laughing. I grinned watching them. This was the real world I wanted.

We all got along in here. And aside from a few moments of Cypress or Atlas refusing a demand from the Collector resulting in our collective punishment, it was nice here. I could feel myself becoming attached to these people and that terrified me. I knew it was only a matter of time before I got traded again, though this Collector seemed more excited about my powers than any others.

In the past my powers were used to disguise things from others. My Collectors had used them for their own purposes the way my current one did. Maybe that was a good thing for him. Giving him a daily break away in his happy place meant something to him. Maybe, just maybe, he'd keep me for it. It gave me a little hope.

I'd lost count of just how many collections I'd been in over the years, and I wasn't even certain how long it had been as it was hard to track days, weeks, and especially years while on the inside.

I had only caught a glimpse of actual daylight once since I was first taken. That was when I'd been moved here. Most of the Collectors relocated us in the dark of night. I'd always loved looking up at the stars. There was something magical about it. But this time I'd been moved during the day, and while the bright sun had hurt my eyes, I'd relished in the warmth of it. It had brought back memories of my childhood that I had long since forgotten.

Aside from that one time, the only sun I saw was on the TV or a scene I manufactured for myself, which was something I rarely did.

It would be easy for me to escape within my own powers. At first, I'd tried that, and it had helped. Doing so had even helped me understand my capabilities better. It also helped me to extend the time of which I could hold onto an image without wearing myself out.

But it had just been a mirage—fake, not real—just like me. The distraction from my life hadn't made me feel any better though

I'd become addicted to it for a while as a teenager. It was so much easier to just hide away when things got tough. It never changed anything though.

Things didn't start to change for me until I changed my attitude about my life. It hadn't been easy, but it had been necessary.

I couldn't control things that had happened to me. But I could choose how I responded to them. Instead of worrying about all the things I wished I'd done or could go back and change, I focus on the now instead. What I can do to make today better than yesterday.

Since coming here, it had been easy to see a little good in life. He gave us a bit more freedom than anywhere else I'd lived. He actually let us spend time together each day, and that meant a lot to me. I had friends now, a family again.

I knew I shouldn't get attached, but I couldn't help it. And I wasn't sure how I'd handle the day I moved to my next collection. For the moment, I just prayed that day didn't come anytime soon.

"Mirage, do you want to play Scrabble with me?" Gwen asked hopefully.

I smiled. "Sure. Let me put my breakfast tray up and I'll be right there."

# Colin

## Chapter 3

I awoke with an unbearable pain shooting through my stomach. Jumping out of bed, I ran to the bathroom and threw up. As I sank to my knees, I unloaded the rest of what was probably last night's dinner. I felt awful, but I knew I wasn't sick.

Reaching for my phone, I dialed Lachlan's number.

"No, you aren't doing this to me again. Get your ass in my office now."

"You don't understand, I'm sick. I just threw up."

"Then carry a barf bag, but you are not canceling another session. Michael is getting impatient. Patrick and Kyle are even talking about it. You have to do this, Colin."

I groaned. "I feel like shit."

"That's okay. You can feel like shit here, or I can come to you even."

I scowled. I hadn't thought about that scenario, and he hadn't offered before. This was the fifth time I'd called it off in a week, but the first that I was legitimately feeling awful.

"You know what? Let's do that. I'm on my way now. Do you want me to pick anything up to settle your stomach?" I could tell by the tone of his voice that he didn't believe me. "Perhaps some pickled pig's feet or boiled eggs?"

My stomach lurched and I threw up again just at the thought.

"Oh shit. You really are sick."

"That's what I tried telling you."

I wiped my mouth with a discarded towel lying on the floor and moaned. I felt miserable.

"How much did you drink last night?"

"Nothing. I think it's something I ate."

"Stay put. I'll call Micah and we'll come to you."

"Sure," I said, feeling too miserable to even argue with him.

After throwing up two more times, I felt a little better, or at least better enough that I was convinced I wasn't going to die today.

My mind drifted off to the dark place again. Maybe dying wouldn't be so bad. I certainly couldn't get my team shot if I wasn't around.

I shook my head. No good came from that line of thinking.

Managing to take a quick shower, I was freshly dressed and toweling off the water from my hair when Lachie arrived with Micah.

"Come in," I told them when I answered the door, then sat down on the couch.

Micah took a seat next to me while Lachlan sat in the recliner across from us.

"Lachlan says you're not feeling well?" Micah asked.

"I woke up sick to my stomach and threw up a few times," I confessed.

"Have you been drinking? Drugs? Anything?"

"No, of course not. It's a work night."

"Okay then, what did you eat last?"

I shrugged having to think back on that. "I had waffles for dinner."

"Homemade?"

"Frozen."

"That's not likely to give you food poisoning. Did you go to bed sick?"

"No."

"And you had nothing to eat this morning before you got sick?"

"No."

"Has this been happening a lot lately?"

I shrugged. "I get stomach aches, but not like this."

"What were your plans for today?"

I gritted my teeth and stared at Lachlan.

"He had an appointment with me first thing this morning," he explained.

Micah considered this and then nodded. It was clear Lachie had filled him in on some things on the drive over.

"This isn't related," I insisted.

"Maybe, maybe not. I can run some tests if you'd like, but I suspect you have a stomach ulcer. It often comes from worry, fear, and stress."

"I'm not worried, afraid, or stressed," I lied.

"I'm sure the pressures of Delta alone could be contributing to this," he said, and I knew he was placating me. He handed me a bottle of pills. "Here. They aren't prescription or anything but give them a try. My dad still swears by papaya pills for most stomach issues, even an ulcer. See if they help you and call the office for a follow-up next week. I hope you feel better."

"Thanks," I muttered as Micah left.

"Well, since we're here, why don't we just get on with our session?" Lachlan suggested.

I groaned, opened the bottle and popped a few of the pills Micah had left into my mouth and swallowed hard.

"I think those are chewable actually," Lachlan informed me.

"Whatever. Let's just get this over with."

I could already feel my stomach cramping again at the thought.

"Just relax, Colin. Whatever we talk about is just between us."

"Right. Because Michael and Patrick aren't going to ask you for updates on how I'm doing."

"Of course they will, but what they get is a generic report. 'He's doing a lot better.' Or 'We have a few things to work out, but he's fit for work' those sorts of things. No details. That's patient privilege."

"I'm not your damn patient."

He looked at me and I didn't need words to understand I absolutely was his patient.

"I'm just here to help," he insisted. "You've clearly been going through some shit, and it can help to talk to someone. Plus, I'm a great listener."

"I don't need a shrink."

"Maybe, but you do need a friend, and you have a lot of shit to get off your chest whether you believe it or not. Look, I was there, okay. I knew you before and after. I can pinpoint the exact moment of change in you, and I'm worried about you, we all are."

"I don't know what you're talking about."

"Yes, you do. The trajectory of that bullet would have hit you in the head, Colin. You would have died on that last out of territory mission had Linc not acted quickly."

"He took a bullet with my name on it," I blurted out. "You're right, I should have died there."

Lachlan sighed and nodded. "I know, man. I know."

"And Linc was hurt because of me. What if that bullet had been just a few inches over? And he's newly mated. Can you even imagine how that would have affected Christine? That's my fault. I screwed up. I almost cost her a mate and nearly lost my friend."

I didn't want to talk to him, but he seemed to know all my triggers to make me react and talk.

"Christine's tough. She wouldn't have blamed you. She knows the risks of this job. All the mates do. Trust me, many of them come and talk to me. Sure they have their fears too, but they understand the importance of this job. Maybe that's something you've lost focus on."

I was honestly surprised to hear him say he had worked with some of the mates. I didn't exactly know what Lachlan did. He trained with us and went on missions with us. He even had territory duties one day a week. But the rest of the time he seemed to just disappear. Aside from counseling some of the victims Westin Force had rescued over the years, I didn't know what he did, and I wasn't even sure what counseling entailed exactly.

When I didn't respond, he started talking again. The tone of his voice combined with his Australian accent had a soothing quality about it that made me relax a little.

"Since that mission, you've been reserved, pulling away from the team. Sure, you're there in body putting in the work, pushing yourself harder than is necessary, but your fear is evident."

I started to protest, but he held up a hand.

"We're all canines, Colin. We know the scent of fear."

I was horrified to hear that. I could smell fear easily on others, why wouldn't they be able to smell it on me.

"Relax. We get it. Trust me on that. There's a lot of scary things out in this world and the Collector threw us all for a loop. He attacked right here on our turf. Everyone's a bit messed up by it. I'd be more concerned if you weren't afraid."

"I'm not afraid for me," I blurted out. "I'm terrified of getting someone else on the team hurt because of me."

He closed his eyes and ran a hand through his hair.

"I see. I suspected it may be something like this. Survivor's guilt."

"What?"

"You're experiencing survivor's guilt. It's basically when something bad happens and you survive but others don't."

"No one died, Lachie."

"I know, but your mind can't seem to come to terms with the fact that Linc could have died in your place."

I felt raw, emotional, seen, and I hated it.

"I don't want to talk anymore," I said softly, determined to shut him out. I didn't want him to know just how true his words were. I didn't want him to know about the various scenarios that had played through my mind since that day, some of which had my entire team dying at the scene. And I for sure didn't want him to know how I'd wished I'd just died there that day, so I didn't have to carry this guilt every single day.

"Okay," he surprised me by saying. "But we're going to need to continue these sessions. If nothing else, it'll make Michael calm down and get Patrick off his ass. I know there's talk of another upcoming mission. They've tracked down two more Collectors from the information we were able to gather from William Davies, that last Collector we took down."

"I know who he was. I hadn't heard another collection was identified. Why am I just hearing this? Are we going out on mission again with Bravo?"

"We are," he confirmed. "But if you don't get your shit together and get through these sessions so I can honestly tell them you're fit to return to the field, then when the time comes, you'll be left here instead. No one on Delta wants that, and I doubt you do either."

I didn't like what I was hearing. Why hadn't I heard about these new collections? Were they really considering leaving me behind? I'd shown up and pulled my weight on the team. I was there in body even if maybe not in spirit. I was still putting in the work.

"I think I'm going to go for a run," I finally told Lachlan.

"Tomorrow then? My office?"

"Yeah, sure."

Like it or not, I was going to have to endure these sessions with him if that's what it took to prove I was still part of the team.

He didn't stop me when I walked out onto my back porch, stripped out of my clothes, and shifted into my wolf form.

After stretching out the kinks, I took off for the woods at a fast pace.

They might think there was something therapeutic about talking to Lachlan, but running in my fur was a far better medicine for me. The pain I'd been enduring in my stomach slowly subsided. Could my wolf heal an ulcer? I was going to have to talk to Micah about it. But I suspected he could.

I cleared my head and just ran, splashing through the creek behind my house, jumping over rocks and fallen trees, and enjoying the feel of the wind in my fur.

Why hadn't I thought to do this sooner? This was exactly what I needed.

But the second I shifted back into my skin, reality set back in and the feelings of doom began to settle around me once more.

# Mirage

## Chapter 4

"Good morning, my pets."

I cringed. He didn't seem to realize how poor his choice of names for us really was. It was clear he had no idea we could all shift into an animal of some sort. But we weren't pets. Our human sides were in control.

"Good morning, Ned. Would you be so kind as to shift for me today?"

"No," Ned growled back.

He hated being put on the spot like that. To shift on demand was degrading to any of us, even more so than being asked to use our powers. I kept my wolf heavily guarded and never let her out. I wasn't even sure yet what the others were because we never talked about it. But I'd learned along the way that all of us had some sort of animal spirit plus a bit of something extra. That was what made us witches.

Ned on the other hand didn't seem to have any extra powers. He wasn't a witch. Just a shifter. Our Collector had been bamboozled and was too dumb to even know it.

All of my previous collections had been passed down from generation to generation. There were dozens of witches in each, and they seemed to know and understand far more than my current Collector.

I'd heard all sorts of stories over the years. A few of the older witches had taken me under their wings and explained things to me. I knew that being inside was a life sentence. There was no getting out, traded, sure, but it was basically the same life of captivity under a new master.

I couldn't help but wonder how this one came into his money, because I'd seen it before, people paid high dollar for us. It didn't make sense to me. It wasn't like they could just show us off to the world because normal humans would be afraid of us. And why would a person ever want to own another?

With only eight of us in the collection, it was obvious that he was new to the game. Plus, he didn't seem to have a clue that we were all shifters. He truly believed Ned to be special in that regard. It did make me wonder what he would do if he knew we could all turn into his personal little pets, giving him an entire menagerie of animals.

The tension in the air was growing as Ned continued to refuse the Collector's request for him to shift into his fox form where he would literally be treated like a pet. I couldn't imagine how disrespectful that was or how demeaning it would feel to be treated like an animal.

I pushed away the irony of that thought. We lived in cages for the enjoyment of our owner. In some ways I supposed we really were just pets.

"I said, shift," his voice rang out down the hall.

"Screw you," Ned replied.

"Ned, please," Gwen begged.

"Just do it, man," Atlas said.

"You're one to talk. You never comply," Ramona challenged him.

"Enough!" the Collector yelled. "My patience is wearing thin today, my pets, and this will not be tolerated. Ned, show me your fox."

As he stood there in the hallway just outside my door, I could see the look of panic in his eyes. He wasn't going to consent. His resolve was strengthening as his chin jutted out in defiance.

The Collector sighed. "You'll find me a reasonable man and my demands are small and simple, but I will not tolerate defiance. I am in control here. You are nothing more than my pets. If you wish to go down this path, you'll find yourselves traded into new collections where your master may not be as amiable as I. Now shift. I wish to pet my fox."

I cringed and so did Ned. It was beyond disrespectful to our kind. Even though I hadn't been raised in a pack beyond my eighth year of life, I still remembered enough to know how prideful shifters are.

Once it was established that our new Collector had no clue about shifters and what witches truly were, no one would talk about the fact anymore. What would he even do if he knew that he'd been duped into buying Ned who wasn't a witch at all?

I didn't bother to tell him to do it. There was no point, though Gwen begged him to anyway. It was a waste of time. Ned wasn't going to change his mind.

"No?" the Collector asked. "Then you have condemned them all. No food today. You'll remain locked in your cages until further notice. And you can thank Ned for this…"

"It's okay," I whispered just as a paralyzing shock racked my body.

I fell to the floor shaking all over. I could hear their screams, but no sound escaped from me. Tears pricked my eyes and my whole body burned from the shockwaves slamming down my spinal cord.

*It'll be over soon,* I told myself trying to shield myself from the pain.

It was horrific, worse than anything I'd experienced in other collections. The device he'd had installed at the base of my neck was the cause of it all, but I couldn't find a way to remove it on my own. The others wouldn't dare try. They were all too scared of him.

Most of the time he didn't frighten me at all, but in this moment as I laid on the floor withering in pain and unable to control my body, I understood why I should fear him.

I waited and begged my brain to numb the pain, but it was too much, too overwhelming. The shocks of sensations went on and on with no end in sight. I was on the verge of blacking out when my power suddenly escaped me.

One moment I'm lying on the cold stone floor, and the next, I was laying on soft grass with the warm sun shining down on me, the space around me transformed into an old favorite memory of me as a child before I was taken into this world of luxury and torture all rolled into one.

I gave a weak smile as my mother put her hand on her hip and looked down at me sternly, though there was still love and a little humor twinkling in her eyes, just as I remembered. "What are you doing down there, silly girl? Get up."

But I couldn't move. I looked around to see other kids my age running and playing in a field next to a creek. They were laughing and having so much fun. It was an old memory, but it never changed beyond what my mother said to me. It was possibly the last truly happy memory I had.

I wanted to stay there and join them. If I could just stand up, I could go and run with them, maybe even never leave this place again and remain eight years old forever.

Deep down I knew that wasn't possible. I couldn't sustain the image for that long. Eventually it would all disappear again, and my reality would come crashing back in on me.

In the days after I was first bought, I'd spent a great deal of time here. It was a happy memory, and it shielded me from the harsh realities of my life. It had kept me innocent for as long as possible, but eventually I'd been forced to grow up. It had happened far too quickly, but that was just the hand I'd been dealt.

My mother scowled down at me once more.

"Get up, child," she said again as her voice morphed into something else, someone else entirely. "Get up, my pet."

I shivered all over as the vision dissipated until the Collector was staring at me through the door. The moment of punishment was over. I could move my arms and legs again. I was back in control of my own body, but the haunting memories of the trauma I'd just been put through still resonated eerily around me.

"I wish to go to my happy place now. Do not try my patience any more than has already been done today."

My head was heavy as I slowly nodded.

Feeling weak and a little sick to my stomach, I somehow managed to conjure up the image I knew he wanted, though I couldn't hold it for long. Still, that seemed to satisfy him enough as he quietly walked away.

In some ways I felt like a traitor, weak. Why couldn't I be strong enough to stand up to him the way Ned had? What would he have done if I'd refused him too?

I often wondered just how many hits with that thing it would take to kill me once and for all, but I couldn't let that happen.

*I am strong.*

*I am beautiful.*

*I am powerful.*

*I am a fighter.*

*I will survive.*

I chanted these reminders to myself. It was something an old witch had taught me in my very first collection. She'd made me repeat the words every day I was there. I'd been traded again a year later for being obstinate.

My second Collector had broken me of that, but every time he tortured me for refusing a command, I'd reminded myself of these words.

I was far more compliant now, wiser in many ways. I picked my battles, but surrendering my dignity for a better life and more freedom seemed a small price to pay. Still, at times like this, I needed the reminder. I had to believe there was something bigger and better meant for my life, and I just had to hold on a little longer to find out just what that would be.

The sound of silence was perhaps the most deafening sound of all.

The doors weren't unlocked. Breakfast wasn't served. As an eerie quiet hung in the air.

"You should have just shifted for him," Gwen said weakly.

"Then next time, you shift for him," Ned insisted.

No one else said a word as the day passed slowly.

I was grateful he had at least left the television on this time. I passed my time curled up on the couch watching a rerun of Full House. Everyone was so happy. I tried to mirror that in my life. I really did want to be that happy too, but days like this made it difficult to find the good in life and hold on to it.

It made me wonder if people outside our walls were truly that happy, or if like my gifts, it was all merely a mirage. But then I remembered my memory and I knew without a doubt that I'd once been that happy too.

The day passed quietly. I hated days like this. In previous collections I may have welcomed a quiet day to myself, but that was only because of the constant crying, screaming, protests, and torture going on around me. But here I felt like I had a family again and I missed them tremendously.

My stomach was rumbling constantly. Again, in other collections this would be normal, but here he actually fed us on a regular schedule, and it was rare for him to withhold food.

No sooner than I thought that my door opened, and a tray was pushed inside before it was slammed closed again.

"Thank you," I whispered as I ran over and grabbed the plate.

It was just a bowl of oatmeal, not at all the quality of food we were used to eating around here, but it was filling and warm, far better than many meals I'd had over the years.

I happily ate without complaint as the next episode started and I wondered just what the real world was really like now.

# Colin

## Chapter 5

I laid down on the couch in Lachlan's office trying to get comfortable like they always showed on television.

He walked in and laughed at me.

"Well, this is different."

Grumbling, I sat up.

"No, by all means, make yourself at home. You're actually early today."

"I heard a rumor that Bravo has managed to get a time and location on a trading post for the Collectors. Michael already said he was going to leave me behind if I didn't keep to the mandatory sessions schedule you set. So here I am."

Over the last week I'd mostly avoided talking to Lachlan again. There were things about me that he just didn't need to know or need confirmed, because sometimes it felt like he knew me better than I knew myself and that was more than a little freaky.

"So, you want to get back out into the field?"

I wasn't sure how to answer that, so I did the best I could.

"I don't want to be left behind," I told him honestly.

"I'm kind of surprised to hear that."

"Why? I haven't slacked on my job or responsibilities. Not once. I've shown up every day. I've put in the work. I've pulled extra shifts. I'm on territory runs four days a week right now and I'm working with the new volunteers to get them up to speed. Have I been doing a shitty job lately?"

"No. Actually the opposite. You've been working yourself to death this last week and using it as an excuse to avoid our sessions."

I growled. "If I'm doing my job, why the hell do I need these sessions?"

"These sessions aren't really about the ability to put in the work, you know that. It's about your mental health, and I believe you're still struggling with the guilt of Linc taking that bullet for you. You're current obsessive working state only tells me I'm right."

I groaned. "I can't win here. I don't do my job up to standard and people worry. I do my job to the best of my ability and people are still worried. Tell me what the hell I'm supposed to do."

"Talk to me."

"That's it?"

"That's it. It really is that simple. Just talk to me."

"Fine, what do you want to talk about."

"Whatever's on your mind."

I considered that for a moment and then shrugged.

"I don't think Christine and Linc really enjoy the meals I've been cooking for them. I'm considering taking up some culinary classes down the mountain or perhaps watching a few step-by-step tutorials online."

"Why do you feel the need to continue feeding Chris and Linc?"

I scowled, knowing I'd just walked right into that one.

"Isn't that what we're all trying to do?" I deflected.

"No. Maybe right after the mission, but that was a few months ago, Colin."

"So what? We're just supposed to forget about them now?"

"Yes."

"What?"

"You have to let it go and move on, Colin. They do not need or want help. Linc's made a full recovery, and they are trying to settle into their new life as a mated couple. They've got this. They don't need our help anymore."

I sighed. Maybe he was right, but the guilt of it all still pressured me to take action and do something, anything.

"I'll stop sending meals," I conceded.

*Maybe he could use a hand fixing stuff around the house or something instead*, I thought.

"They need time alone. That's it right now. And if there's anything more like stuff around the house he needs help with, then he'll let us know."

I glared at him. "When are you going to admit you're a freaking mind-reading witch?"

He chuckled. "I wish. Would make my job so much easier."

I wasn't convinced at all.

"Tell me, how are you feeling? Are you sleeping?"

"I feel okay, I guess. I'm sleeping as much as usual."

"So barely?"

"I manage a good four hours a night at least."

"I can prescribe you something to help with that."

"Hard pass."

"Is that why you've been working so many long hours lately?"

I shrugged. "Maybe." I looked down at my watch. "Speaking of which, I have to meet up with the volunteer trainees in ten minutes, so I guess this meeting is over."

"Not so fast. I had Michael push it back by two hours."

"What? Why?"

"Because I knew you'd try to weasel out of this using it as an excuse."

I hated that he was right.

"Why don't you just tell me what it is I'm supposed to do or not do and then we can get all of this sorted quickly."

"It's not that simple, Colin. I need you to let go of what happened. I need you to stop overthinking everything, it makes you slow in response time whether you believe it or not. And I need you to be in a better mental state the next time we go out in the field where someone's life could be on the line."

"Fine. Done. And I don't have a slower response time." I mumbled that last part under my breath, but I knew he heard it when he chuckled.

"Just saying it doesn't make it so."

"I still can't win here. What have you heard about the trading post?"

He sighed. "Not much. They're still watching and waiting but there appears to be some activity going on. There could be another trade show coming up soon. That's all I know."

I nodded. "Okay. That's good. I mean in theory these trade shows have several Collectors coming together, right?"

"Yes."

"And we'll be there to collect them instead."

He didn't say anything, but from the look on his face I was pretty sure I wasn't going to get invited along on that mission. Did that go for all of Delta or just me?

"Okay, can we be done for now then? I need to figure out how I'm going to prove to you that I can let this go, stop overthinking it, and get in a better mental state."

"It's not something you can just do, Colin. But it is something I can help you work through. If you'll let me."

"We'll see," I said, not quite ready to commit to that or let go of the guilt I was still harboring.

Thankfully Lachlan conceded to letting me leave. I stopped by Michael's office first.

"Lachie tells me you changed my schedule for training the volunteers today. What time am I supposed to meet with them then?"

Michael looked up from his paperwork and grinned. Then he looked at his watch.

"You have one hour. How'd your session go today?"

"Good."

I knew he was fishing, and I wasn't about to bite.

The truth was that I had no clue what they wanted from me. I couldn't help how I felt. Could I? Logically I knew it wasn't rational but that didn't stop the thoughts from coming. It didn't change the need I had to fix it even though there really wasn't anything to fix.

When I left Michael's office I stopped by the gym. Linc was in there running on one of the treadmills. I quickly changed into shorts and a T-shirt and jumped on the treadmill next to him as I quickly matched his pace.

He grunted and lifted his chin towards me as he sped up the pace.

I grinned to myself but increased mine to match.

We ran in silence for a while. It was nice. Normal. But eventually he surprised me by speaking.

"Hey, Chris wanted me to tell you that the enchiladas you sent over were actually pretty good."

I beamed up at him. "Thanks."

Before I could say anything more, he held up a hand to stop me.

"That's not encouragement for more food. Please. We'll be eating it down for the rest of the year as it is."

I chuckled feeling a little more like my old self today.

"I get it. No more food. But if you need help with anything around the house or whatever, anything at all, just let me know."

He sighed. "You don't have to keep doing this, Colin. If I'd been in those crosshairs, I know without a doubt that you'd have jumped in to save me too."

I gulped hard. We had never come out and really talked about it.

"I know I would, but I hate that you had to take a bullet for me."

"It was just a little flesh wound. Besides, it gave me a couple weeks off duty to spend time with my mate when I needed it most."

He grinned, and I knew that while there was probably a little truth to that, he was also saying it to placate me, and I hated that.

"I don't know how I'm going to react on our next big mission. Every night I dream of a million different ways that day could have gone and it's eating me up inside. I don't know how to let it go. Maybe the others are right to worry. Maybe I'm not cut out for this job after all."

"Shut the hell up," Linc said as he looked around to ensure no one was listening.

I looked over at him, surprised by the tone of his voice.

"The team needs you out there, Colin. I need you out there. There is no one else I trust more to have my back than you."

"I could have gotten you killed."

"Coulda, shoulda, woulda. I know you, and I know you aren't going to rest until you find a way to redeem yourself, and that means I'm safer than ever with you by my side. Just don't get yourself killed trying to make things right in your mind. And it is all in your mind."

"Don't you think I know that?"

"Have you talked to Lachlan about all of this?"

"Some." But I knew I'd never opened up to him the way I was with Linc now.

"He's a good man. He can help you if you let him."

"I don't know how to let him. I don't know how to meet his expectations or how to change the way I feel. This darkness and feeling of doom surrounding me is crushing enough without trying to explain it to him."

He nodded. "I told him you were depressed. I've been there, man. Keep aiming for the light. Someday it'll all be better, and this will just be a forgotten nightmare."

I wanted to press him and hear his story, but I didn't dare. It felt too intrusive.

"Look, in our line of work we see some of the best of people but also the worst. It's easy to let your mind screw with you, but you're stronger than that too. You know damn well that any one of us would have taken that bullet to save you. And we all know you wouldn't hesitate to do the same. You would have been relieved of duty weeks ago if any of us thought that wasn't still the case. Depression lies to you. It makes you think unrealistic things. Stop listening to it."

"It's not that easy."

"Oh, I know, but as long as you keep fighting it, you're going to be okay. Eventually. Or as okay as you ever were at least. So maybe not entirely normal or anything." He gave me a sheepish grin.

I shook my head and upped the speed on my treadmill to run much faster.

"Oh, it's going to be like that, is it?"

He matched my pace, but he was no longer talking. Come to think of it, this may have been the most I'd ever heard Linc actually talk and open up. He gave me a lot to think about. It wasn't anything I didn't already know but hearing it from him somehow resonated a little differently, and in a weird way it felt like just a bit of the weight bearing down on me had been lifted.

# Mirage

## Chapter 6

"Good morning, my pets."

I awoke with a groan. It wasn't like me to sleep in. Either that or he was early this morning. I had no real way to tell. There were no clocks around and no windows to the outside world.

It made me feel groggy and a little uneasy.

"Good morning, Mirage. Today is a very special day for you. Get up. I need you showered and dressed in this."

He opened the door and walked in with a long box. I hesitantly took it and opened it to find a beautiful red dress inside.

I gulped hard. One of my past Collectors used to give girls gifts like this before he took them away and did unspeakable things to them. That was how I'd learned all about sex at the ripe age of ten.

I shuddered at the thought. I'd kill him if he tried to lay a hand on me or die trying.

The horror must have been evident on my face because he took a step back.

"We're going on a little trip today. You'll be the shiniest pet in the room. Now get ready. I'll be back in an hour to collect you."

He dropped the box onto my bed and turned to leave without another word.

I stood there in shock as understanding seeped in. I was being traded today and he wanted me to look my best.

Unshed tears stung my eyes.

Why? I'd done everything he asked, I thought as I numbly stripped and stepped into the shower. I liked it here. And what would Ramona, Cypress, Gwen, Ned, Boris, Atlas, and Mags do without me? We were like family.

My heart was breaking as I prepared myself for the inevitable. I knew this day would come eventually but I wasn't ready. This felt like a complete blindside.

I put on the gown he'd brought me. I had to admit it was beautiful. I'd never worn such a thing before. When I twirled it swished around me like a princess dress. I hated that I loved it.

Finding the door to my room unlocked and hearing sounds of laughter down the hallway, I left my room and walked down to the cafeteria.

The room fell silent as I entered.

Mags gasped and shook her head.

Cypress started to cry.

Atlas punched the table, nearly breaking it in two.

"He can't do this," Ned protested.

I tried to stay strong even when Gwen jumped up and ran to hug me.

"It's going to be okay," she whispered.

"But why her?" Boris asked. "Ned was the one that defied him. Mirage has always been his favorite. Why her?"

"This sucks," Ramona said. "For the most part, I like it here. I don't want to lose any of you."

"I agree with Ramona. You're all like family to me," Ned added.

I bit my lip to keep from crying and nodded.

"We need to stand up to him. He can't do this," he continued.

"You tried that yesterday and look where it left us," Gwen told him as she glared at him.

"I'm sorry. I just couldn't play his game. It's insulting. He's not even smart enough to know I shouldn't be here."

We all nodded, knowing it was true.

Breakfast took a solemn turn as I got my food and sat down with the others. We pulled all the tables together this time. One big family. It nearly broke my heart as I tried to stay strong for them.

Atlas was usually the quieter one amongst us, but he was the one who opened up first. "Okay, here's the plan. When he comes for you, Boris will move a chair in place and force him to sit. Cypress will create vines and secure him to the chair."

"I'll keep him calm so he can't call for help or fight us," Gwen offered.

"He's allergic to magnolias. Ironic, huh? I'll conjure up some big ones to make him miserable," Mags said with a grin.

"And since he wants to see my fox so badly, I'll shift and bite him," Ned added.

"If you're willing to disguise us, Atlas can carry him right out as I forge a path for us, or preferably, Atlas can just punch his lights out and we all just leave together and never look back," Ramona suggested.

I frowned. "The chips he implanted. I mean, isn't that what's keeping us here as it is?"

It was true that between the lot of us we could easily escape this place, but he would make us suffer for it.

"How far do you think his reach goes?" Mags asked.

Cypress shrugged. "After yesterday, I'm not sure I'm ready to chance it."

"But we can't just let him trade Mirage," Ned protested.

"He often carries it on him. We'll take it when we leave," Boris suggested.

We were seriously starting to consider this plan when the Collector walked in.

"Good morning, pets. Today's an exciting day. We may have some new faces joining us very soon."

He was gleeful, practically buzzing with excitement.

"Say goodbye, Mirage. We're going to be late."

When he grabbed my arm, it was clear he was just saying the words and had no intention of allowing me to properly say goodbye to my friends.

They all started to protest. I watched as the stick he used to trigger our chips began shaking in his hand.

"Boris, enough!" he barked. "I will not have such dissension. You know better."

"You can't trade her," Boris yelled.

"I am your master, and I can do whatever I bloody well feel like."

He grabbed me by the arm hard. I cried out from the pain of his grip as he dragged me from the room.

The plan was forgotten. No one dared make a move to save me as our master ominously held out the trigger threatening to drop us all to our knees with the push of a button. I'd never felt so weak and useless as I did in that moment.

"Goodbye," I whispered weakly as he pushed me down the hall stopping at the large metal door that he opened and shoved me through.

When I'd arrived, I'd been blindfolded. It was a normal precaution so that we wouldn't learn the route out should an escape be attempted. But with the chaos and threat of the morning, he wasn't thinking and didn't take any of the usual precautions as he walked me outside.

My eyes stung from the bright sunlight, and I tried to cover them, making me stumble and fall to the ground.

I could smell the blood from my skinned knee that now burned with the familiarity of a memory long forgotten.

"Get up," he ordered, pulling me back to my feet.

My eyes were starting to adjust to the light of day, and I took a moment to look around and get my bearings straight.

I realized that we weren't being kept in some dungeon or hidden room at all. We were simply in a small building on the outskirts of a farm. From the outside it looked like a small barn, though inside those walls were fortified with steel. All around were open fields, cows, and sheep.

My heart sank as I realized there was nowhere to hide, nowhere to run should we have attempted an escape. I could hide us but that would drain me. Atlas would have to carry me out to conserve my energy.

I would tell them, warn them… if I were to return to this place.

A short distance away there was a black SUV waiting for us. Someone jumped out of the front seat and opened the back door. The Collector shoved me in ahead of him as I quickly scooted to the far side.

"Put your seatbelt on," he ordered.

I quickly obeyed.

Everything inside me screamed to rebel. Run! Do something. But I was frozen.

Where would I go? What would I do? I knew nothing about the real world. It was more than a little terrifying. In some weird way, it was safer, comfortable even, being in a collection. I understood the rules there and knew how to survive. Out here? I was clueless.

Staring out the window I watched as the landscape changed around us from fields and farms to a small town and then into a city.

The buildings were huge. I never even imagined such a place as I watched in shock as they only grew bigger the closer we got. They towered over us blocking out the sun.

"Where are we?" I whispered.

"Chicago," the Collector surprised me by saying.

I didn't dare ask any further questions. Eventually we went under the city and the car stopped and parked. As I got out, I looked around surprised to see tents set up in between the streets. Faces peeked out to look at us and then quickly disappeared again.

The Collector stopped and looked me over. He smoothed out my dress and then nodded.

"You look lovely."

I stayed quiet trying not to show how upset I was at being traded so soon.

He escorted me inside. It was fancy, glamorous even. Everyone was dressed up. I didn't even remotely look out of place. I'd never seen a trading show like it before.

From my experience they cleaned us up and then kept us in cages. I never even really saw the Collectors bidding on me until after the transaction was complete. At some point I would be moved into a room covered in mirrors. They would tell me to perform.

It was weird watching myself use my powers. And I knew I couldn't create a mirage for myself. I had to project outward instead, something for them to all see.

At some point a person would return and take me away again. I'd wait in a cage in the back with dozens, sometimes hundreds of other witches just waiting until my new master came to collect me.

It wasn't until we walked over to a wall and the lights came on that I realized I was on the other side of the mirrored box.

Inside there was a woman standing there looking confused and scared.

"Show us your powers," an announcer said.

I didn't need the power of an empath to know she was sad and terrified as she sent fireworks up towards the ceiling as they exploded and twinkled down around her.

Everyone watching cheered and clapped.

"Why me? Why are you trading me?" I finally cracked and asked.

"Oh, my sweet pet. I wouldn't dream of trading you. I merely wish to show you off."

My heart soared. "Really?"

"Absolutely. You have nothing to fear. If you were being traded, you wouldn't be on this side of the wall."

I cringed, knowing he was right.

Looking around the room I was relieved that I didn't see any of my former Collectors present as we mingled around the room.

"Luther, come over here. I want to introduce you to my new friend. The two of you should get along famously. He's new to collecting as well. Allow me to introduce Mr. Walter Grimes and his beautiful bride, Tayla."

The woman smiled at me but there was a tightness to it and a slight confusion too. I sniffed the air and nearly gasped. They were shifters, wolves even. I was certain of it.

"And who is this?" I heard her mate ask as I realized I'd tuned out their conversation entirely from the shock of two wolf shifters collecting witches. It was beyond disgusting.

"Oh, pay her no mind. I promise she'll cause no harm here, will you, my pet. This is Mirage, my most prized possession."

The man who had made the introductions scoffed. "And you just allow her to roam free amongst us."

"Trust me, my friend, she knows her place and I have her well-handled. If she steps out of line, it's nothing more than the push of button to regain full control."

His smile sickened me.

"I'm afraid we can't just take your word on that. What is her power?"

"Much like her name, Mirage is capable of wonderous illusions. Show him, my pet."

I didn't hesitate. Something told me it would not be good if I put up a fight now. Instead, I transported those closest to us into my master's favorite vision.

"Wow."

"Amazing."

"It really feels as if we've just been transported to Aruba."

"It's fabulous, isn't it?" Luther gloated as I allowed my powers to recede.

"That was certainly something to be proud of, but how can we be certain she won't transport us again and just leave us there."

I wanted to tell him he was being ridiculous. That wasn't how my powers worked, but I bit my tongue knowing no good could come of it.

"Alistair, you wound me. I would never put any of you in danger. She's perfectly harmless, I assure you."

"And we just take your word on that?" a woman listening in nearby said.

"Ravenna, calm down. I'm sure he has a good reason for breaking protocol like this."

"What protocol?" Luther asked.

It was funny. I never would have pegged my Collector as a Luther. It just didn't seem to quite fit him. I'd never known of the others' names. To me they were all just blank nameless faces.

Ravenna groaned and rolled her eyes. "These new Collectors don't know shit about our ways. As his sponsor it's your job to teach him these things, Alistair."

"Sorry Luther. It's not customary to bring our pets out in public, especially to an event like this."

"Oh. My sincere apologies. I did not know."

"We've had issues before. You think you have her under your control, but you can't trust them no matter how well behaved she may appear."

I looked up just in time to see the thinly veiled mask on Tayla's face slip. There was fury in her eyes. Walter nudged her and she immediately transitioned back to character. Was this just an act for them? What were they doing here? I had a million questions I wanted to ask them. Starting with why were shifters buying up witches?

"I'm afraid we're going to have to move her to a cage until you're ready to go unless you can give us absolute verification that you have her under control," Alistair said.

Ravenna snorted. "And we know that's impossible."

Luther turned to me. "My apologies, dear. You have done nothing wrong. I'll try to make this quick."

I wasn't sure what he was talking about until it was too late. He held up the trigger and pressed the button.

Falling to my knees, I cried out in pain as shocks ran down my spine.

I was pretty sure I didn't imagine the look of horror Walter and Tayla shared, or the way his hand gripped her arm when she took a step towards me. It was clear they didn't approve of this torture. Why wouldn't they intercede and help me?

The pain subsided much faster than usual, but it took me a moment still to catch my breath and regain control of my limbs.

Alistair started a round of applause as I was still sprawled out across the floor having drawn the attention of everyone in the room.

"What is this?" Ravenna asked in wonder.

"All state-of-the-art. Spared no expense. Each of my treasures have been outfitted with a device attached directly to their spinal cords. I alone hold the trigger to activate it. It doesn't hurt them in the least. It's more akin to a taser and feels similar."

"Can you isolate which witch you shock at any given time?" she asked curiously.

"The technology is there for that. I chose just one trigger. I believe collective punishment ensures a stronger bond and better commitment to the collection."

"Clearly you have a small collection," she countered with a laugh. "Can you even imagine?"

Luther's cheeks brightened and I could sense his anger and embarrassment at having been called out like that.

"Perhaps, but he's certainly on to something, especially if the signals can be isolated," Alistair said with interest.

"Ladies and gentleman, let us begin."

# Colin

## Chapter 7

I awoke with a jolt in a pool of sweat. Scrubbing my face
with my hands, I jumped out of bed and ran to the bathroom fearing
I was about to throw up.

I'd been battling nightmares a lot since the incident. It came
with the depression. This wasn't my first battle in this dark place.

This one had been so real though and left me feeling helpless
and scared.

No one had died this time, but there had been this girl that
we'd had to leave behind. I couldn't save her, and I didn't know if
she was dead or alive. Her face haunted me even after waking.

I could see her so vividly. Sometimes she looked terrified,
and other times she just looked disappointed in me. I hated that look
the most. It left me with an unsettled feeling as I jumped in the
shower and prepared to start my day.

Today I was working with Lane, our new Sheriff. He was a
young guy but seemed to truly care about the job and his part in
keeping San Marco safe.

Even knowing I was much too early, I showed up at his
office anyway. I wasn't surprised to find him there working already.

He glanced up from some paperwork on his desk and grinned.

"Hey, Colin. Come on in. I'm just wrapping up here."

"Sorry I'm early. Couldn't sleep."

He gave me a sympathetic look and nodded.

"I've been there. I get it."

"What are you talking about?" I asked.

"I know what happened with you and Linc on your last mission."

I groaned.

"Does everyone in the freaking Pack know about that?"

He shrugged. "Patrick wanted me kept in the loop when you were assigned to help out with my department."

There was no way this kid had any clue what I was going through.

Chuckling, he pushed the stack of files to the side.

"I know. Shocking, right. You're already aware that I'm an outsider. I didn't grow up here in Westin. I transferred. I'm actually a city boy. My original pack is from the Chicago area, and I was with Chicago PD prior to coming here. I lost my partner in a shootout. He didn't just take a bullet for me; he died in the process. What I wouldn't give to have traded places with him."

I couldn't believe what I was hearing. He really did understand, probably more than anyone else I knew.

"So, yeah, I've been there. I know how your mind can twist that into ugly scenarios that leave you crippled."

"How did you get through it?"

He shrugged. "A lot of counseling."

I cringed thinking of Lachlan.

The look on my face made him laugh.

"I know. I wasn't thrilled with it either, but when I finally started opening up and talking about it, it was better. Didn't change anything, but it did help me work through those feelings. I was even suicidal at my worst. Survivor's guilt is what they called it."

I hadn't really considered killing myself, but I knew that if it happened while protecting my team, I would be okay with it too. Did that make me somewhat suicidal?

"That's what Lachlan calls it for me too."

He nodded. "Even though Linc survived, I'm sure the emotions of it all are similar. And man, those what ifs are the worst."

I nodded in agreement.

"Sometimes I can't even fully function because of them."

"How'd you get past it all?"

He chuckled. "There's no truly getting past it, Colin. You just learn to carry it with you. I stayed for two years and got back to active duty before hearing there was an opening here and taking it. The change of pace has helped a lot, but don't think I'm just okay. I'm not. I may never be, but I'm functional and I'm no longer suicidal. I found a new purpose and I'm at peace with that."

Peace? I couldn't even remember what that felt like anymore.

"Nightmares," I blurted out. "I have these nightmares and the emotions of them seem to linger throughout the day. I don't know how to stop them."

"Face them."

"Huh?"

"Face them. What was your nightmare about?"

"This one was different from the others. Usually it's someone on my team dying and I can't stop it. But this one was a girl who was being held captive and I couldn't save her."

"That makes sense. And that's good."

"How is that good?"

"Because your nightmare shifted from the trauma of what you experienced to another probable scenario of the job."

"Great, so now I'm contaminating the entire job?"

He grinned and shook his head. "I don't think so. Tell me, how does it make you feel right now that you didn't save her before you woke?"

"Terrible. I almost went back to sleep and tried to force an ending change, because I felt so helpless. That never worked before though."

"Never did for me either. I think you probably should just face it head on. The others will be worried sick about you and monitor your every movement. It's going to be annoying but jumping back on the saddle helped me more than I ever imagined."

I found that hard to believe given he'd packed up and moved halfway across the country, even switching Pack allegiances in the process. But I didn't say so.

Maybe I'd never be okay, but just maybe that was okay too. I couldn't erase what happened or how it affected me. I just had to find a way to live with it.

"Why don't we postpone things today. I have plenty of busy work for the guys. We can arrange training another day."

"I need to work, Lane. Staying busy helps."

"So does sitting with this and coming to terms with what happened. Trust me you'll be stronger for it and ready to jump back into field work when the time comes."

"I'm not sure if that's going to happen or not. What if I just can't do it anymore?"

"Trust me. You can."

I took his offer to blow off our morning plans, but I didn't know if I really believed what he said or not. It certainly had given me a lot to think about, though.

In the end it hadn't mattered if I was ready or not. Bravo team had been sent out for the trade show mission and only Walker had been invited along to join them. He and Taylor had been sent inside, undercover. With the money they had for the auction they were able to buy the freedom of three witches.

"It's not enough," Taylor argued during our combined debriefing.

"We couldn't just buy them all up even if we'd had the funds to do so," Walker argued. "That would have only looked suspicious and painted a target on our backs. Now, we're in T. Slow and steady, we'll get them all."

"How many were there?" Michael asked.

"About three dozen," Tarron told him.

"We only saved three out of thirty-six?" I asked feeling sick at the thought.

"Exactly," T said. "And then what about poor Mirage? I wanted to kick Luther's ass for what he did to her."

"What happened?" Tucker asked.

"Luther Carrington. He's new to the game and likes to show off. He brought one of his girls along with him, made her demonstrate her powers, and then when concern was voiced, he showed us all the new state-of-the-art tracking device and torture system he had installed in her," Walker said.

It made my blood boil hearing him talk.

"This device is attached to their spinal cords and with the click of a button it's like hitting them with a high capacity taser right down their nervous systems," he explained.

"It was horrific. Walker had to hold me back from blowing our cover," Taylor confessed. "I've never felt so helpless having to stand there and just watch it happen. My vote goes to taking Luther Carrington down first. I know he's insignificant in the big scheme of things. He didn't even add to his collection, just paraded around his *"most prized treasure"* as he calls her. So we should be able to get in and back out quickly. I just cannot stand the thought of her stuck in there with that threat hanging over her head for even a second longer."

"As you can see, Taylor was very affected by this mission," Grant said as he wrapped a protective arm around his mate.

"She knew we were imposters. The look of disgust and disappointment on her face knowing two shifters were there shopping for a collection will haunt me until we make this right. I have to save Mirage."

"Mirage? That's her name?" I asked.

"Yeah. I'm guessing it's based on her powers. She has the ability to conceal things by showing an image so realistic that you'd swear you were just transported. She gave us a demonstration and it was pretty amazing," Walker explained.

"They both feel pretty strongly about this," Silas said with a sigh. "We certainly have much bigger fish to fry, but I feel like we need to give them this. It's personal at this point."

"Okay," Michael said. "Just tell us what you need from Delta."

"We know it's a small collection, but we aren't certain exactly how small we're talking here," Painter began.

"Thanks to Taylor's obsession with this one, we were able to put a bug on the car. It's a local-to-the-area collection based in Wisconsin. Unlike many of the others, we suspect this guy keeps his collection in an isolated area out on his farm. Satellite tracking points to a large barn on the property. He went there first from the trade show, so we're assuming he dropped Mirage off there before going home. That's just an assumption though. We could arrive and find there's nothing but cows there," Tarron informed us.

"It's worth the risk to find out," Taylor insisted.

"We don't know exactly how many we're talking here," Silas said.

"So we go in with a full team then?" I asked.

There were some worried looks shot my way, and I feared they were going to bench me on this mission. I couldn't explain why, but if Delta was going in, I had to be there. As terrified as I was of getting someone else hurt, I was suddenly more afraid of not being there to save them.

I was going to do whatever it took to be there.

"Um, yeah," Jake said hesitantly. "Or at least Silas and Michael will discuss and determine who's doing what and then let us know."

Great. I knew then that even Bravo team was aware of my struggles and that did not make me happy. They weren't leaving me out of this mission, and I was going to do everything possible to make sure of that.

As soon as the meeting was adjourned, I rounded on Michael.

He held up a hand and motioned for me to follow him down to his office. He didn't speak until the door was closed behind him.

"Don't leave me behind on this. I can do it."

"Can you?"

"Look, I know everyone is worried about me and I've sulked and struggled with some dark thoughts since the last mission. I'm dealing with it."

"Are you?"

"Yes. And the faster I get back out there the better I'll be."

"Colin, I can't count on that. The guys don't trust you right now and that's more dangerous than anything."

"I've never given you or anyone else here reason not to trust me. Depression is real, Michael, and every single one of you would be lying assholes if you said you've never experienced it before. You almost need a bit of that edge in this job. Okay, I freaked out over Linc getting hurt when it should have been me. At least give me the chance to pay him back for that."

A laugh behind me jolted me and I turned around to see Lachlan sitting there. I scowled at him.

"That's the most real thing I've heard you say yet."

I wanted to punch the smug look off his face.

"I'm not making this decision," Michael surprised me by saying. "Your therapist is, so you have about twelve hours to convince him that you're capable of handling this mission before we roll out."

I nodded. "Fine. I'm on perimeter detail today and need to get my run in before we go. Come on, Lachie. We don't have time to waste."

He grinned but followed.

We didn't talk as we walked out of headquarters, took the elevator up to the Lodge that was used as a cover for our location, and then finally outside.

"Hop in," I told him.

"Why the sudden change?" he asked.

"It's not a change," I lied.

"Yeah, it is. You just opened up to Michael, and I can sense that you are more resolved and ready to do this."

I sighed. "Lane."

"Huh?"

"The new Sheriff. Lane Stoddard. I was supposed to work with him and his team this morning. We talked instead."

Lachlan nodded like he understood what I meant.

"Why hadn't I thought about that sooner?"

"You knew?"

"About Stoddard? Of course. He was assigned to me the second he arrived. Did he tell you why?"

"Yeah. Survivor's guilt. The same thing you claim I have."

"I'm glad you two talked."

"Me too," I confessed.

I wasn't entirely ready to open up to Lachie the way I had Lane, but this time when he tagged along on my perimeter run, I didn't go out of my way to run faster and lose him. Instead, I kept a steady pace as he easily fell into step beside me.

Oddly, that alone felt like progress, and by the time we got back to headquarters, I felt just a little more like the old me.

"I'm going to recommend you for the mission. The progress you've made today is huge. I'm really proud of you, Colin."

His praise shouldn't have felt so damn good, but it did. Still, it paled in comparison to the relief his words gave me. I was being given a second chance, and I wasn't going to blow it or give anyone reason to worry about me again.

# Mirage

## Chapter 8

I awoke feeling groggy and out of sorts. It took me a moment to get my bearings straight. I was in my room and the dress I'd worn to the trade show was draped over my little couch. It had all been real.

Jumping out of bed, I ran to the toilet and vomited. I was still there puking when Atlas came into my room to check on me.

"Hey, are you okay?" he asked as he pulled my hair back and rubbed my back.

"No. I'm not okay," I admitted.

"What happened? We thought you were being traded."

"So did I. Instead, he just dressed me up and paraded me around to all his new rich friends. It was humiliating. And then I had to just sit there and smile, Atlas, while they forced those captured to perform in the box as they were sold off to the highest bidder. I think it's even worse feeling helpless and just sitting there watching, unable to do anything to stop it. I'd have rather been put in the box and sold off myself than to witness that."

Tears stung my eyes as I recounted the terrifying look in the eyes of a young girl with water powers who had gone at a premium to that traitor wolf shifter and his mate.

"One of the buyers was a shifter."

"What? That can't be right."

"I know what I smelled. He and his mate were wolves. It was beyond disgusting. How could they?"

"I don't understand how anyone with even the slightest bit of humanity can do this to others. Every single one of them are more animalistic than any of us will ever be."

I could sense his anger, too.

"I didn't hear the Collector come through this morning."

"Because he didn't."

"Really? Why?"

"How the hell are we supposed to know? It's a first though."

"Luther. His name is Luther," I blurted out.

Somehow knowing his real name felt like a new sort of power.

"He told you that?"

"Of course not, but in a room full of Collectors, they don't just call each other the Collector."

"It could be a fake name," he pointed out.

I shrugged. "Regardless, it somehow humanized him more to me. He's just a man, Atlas, an asshole for sure, but no different than any of us."

He snorted. "I can list dozens of ways he's different from us, and not just the obvious ones, but I get what you're saying."

I laid there contemplating throwing up again, but my stomach was slowly settling.

"Are you okay?" he finally asked.

"I think so."

I was still shaky and a little nauseous, but I didn't think I was going to vomit anymore.

"Probably not the best time to mention it, but we saved you a plate of breakfast if you want to try and eat something."

Nodding, I started to get up, but Atlas jumped up and assisted me.

"Thanks," I muttered.

Normally I would stubbornly refuse his help for fear it made me look weak, but at that moment all pride was gone.

He gave me a moment to myself to change and freshen up and then helped me down the hall where the others were waiting for us.

No one asked me to recount things, but Atlas filled them in on what I'd told him. Several were arguably angry while the others were just upset.

I managed to get a few bites in me before a memory crossed my mind.

"Hey, last night, did any of you feel the pain?"

"What do you mean?" Mags asked.

"You know, the pain from the clicker that the device he implanted in us causes."

They all shook their heads, and I sighed in relief.

"He used that on you?" Ned asked with a growl.

I nodded. "When they discovered what I was people started to freak out. To prove he had me under control, he gave a demo."

Cypress gasped.

"In front of everyone?" Gwen asked.

"Right in the middle of the room."

"That's humiliating," Boris whispered.

"It was, but I'm so glad none of you were affected."

"That means it's short-ranged," Ramona said. "That's good information to have."

"Did you see anything outside? Like what's around us? Where in the house are we?" Magnolia asked.

As I started feeling better and finished eating, I recounted everything I'd seen on the little trip.

"We're in the middle of a field?" Atlas asked.

"Yup. I saw nothing but fields around us."

He shared a look with Ramona and nodded. I knew they weren't telepaths, yet they somehow seemed to be speaking silently to each other.

"We can get out of here then," Ramona said confidently.

"Now?" Cypress asked.

"No, we need to buy a little more time and prepare. I need to ensure I can get out and see what's on the other side for myself. I can only carry one person at a time through."

"There are cameras everywhere," Boris mentioned. "But I can slowly move them so they aren't angled directly at the door."

"And when you're ready, I think I can mask the hallway to make it appear that you aren't there. I'm not a hundred percent certain how that works through cameras though so there's a fifty-fifty chance it'll work. That's why I've never suggested it before. I worry that my mirage won't show through the cameras the way it does in person. I think it should, just a little paranoia on my part."

Ned shrugged. "It's worth a try. And if we cause a bit of a disturbance at the same time, if someone is watching they'll be distracted. Hopefully."

"That's a great idea, Ned," Gwen said.

"Guys, are we seriously going to do this?" Cypress asked. "I don't want to get my hopes up yet, but do you really think we could do it?"

The thought of leaving terrified me. I had no idea what awaited us in the real world. This was all I knew, but after what I'd experienced, I was ready to take that risk.

"Let's wait and see if the normal routine goes back into effect. He obviously didn't buy any new witches this time," Atlas said, taking control of the situations. "Baby steps. We only have one shot at this, and it needs to be perfect. Boris, start slowly repositioning the cameras, very small movements, nothing drastic."

We all agreed.

There was a lot of anxious energy and fear around the room, but also excitement.

Could we really get out of this place?

*****

A few days passed and when nothing further happened aside from the Collector returning and our normal routine being reinstated, the overall mood tanked. We were never getting out of here. My morale was at an all-time low as I carried the memories of what had happened with me while being stuck.

It was as if a massive change had shifted inside me, yet I was helpless to evoke the actual changes I desperately wanted to see.

"Good morning, my pets," I awoke with a groan.

He'd put on a new movie for this month called Groundhog Day. I realized quickly just how accurate that movie was to my real life as I relived the same day over and over. Nothing ever changed. His morning greeting was nothing more than a stabbing reminder of that fact.

"Why the long face, Mirage?" Gwen asked.

"Yeah, you're usually the most optimistic of all. What's wrong?" Cypress asked.

I shrugged. Where to even begin to explain my frustrations.

The brief moment of hope had come crashing down on me in the most depressing way. We were never getting out of here. The best I could hope for in life was to stay here with these people I genuinely cared about. Beyond that there was nothing for me in this life.

In all my years of captivity I'd never allowed myself to think about it or wallow in this fact, but it was time to face the music. This is my life.

No sooner had I thought it, the door burst open and the Collector ran in.

"Mirage!" he yelled out.

He was out of breath and red-faced when he came into the room.

"What's wrong?" I asked.

"We only have seconds." He shoved a picture into my hands. "Make this place look like this from the door and beyond. Stupid inspector wants to see every building and he's headed this way now. Hurry!"

Atlas shook his head behind me begging me not to do it.

I was well aware of the fact that this could be our chance of escape.

Luther must have sensed my hesitation as he pulled out the pen-like stick from his pocket and twirled it between his fingers.

"Don't even think of defying me. He is human and will only send you to a lab to be researched. He won't appreciate you the way I do, but one step out of line and you'll force me to do something I don't want to do."

I sighed and transformed the room, leaving him on the outside while keeping me and my friends behind the curtain.

"Why?" Atlas asked shooting me a disappointed look.

"You heard him," Gwen whispered.

As a man walked into the room seeing exactly what I wanted him to see, he smiled and looked around as he checked something off of a clipboard.

It was working. I'd never pushed my powers so wide and held them for so long before. As they stood there and talked, I didn't think they would ever leave.

I watched as Cypress edged towards the door. She was going to make a run for it.

Suddenly the room was filled with apprehension, and I realized it was Gwen projecting on everyone. The humans certainly felt the shift in the room as the inspector shook his pen against his clipboard and loosened his collar.

"Is it a little stuffy in here? How about we move on to the next barn," he suggested seconds before Cypress reached the door.

They left quickly as she shot Gwen an angry look and I let the facade drop.

"You did that on purpose, Gwen. I could have made it."

"And then what?" Ned asked. "Is he the only one here for the inspection? You had no idea what you'd be walking into and without Mirage's cover you would have been fully exposed the second to you breeched the door."

She yelled in frustration.

We were all feeling it.

"I thought the goal was to get out of here. We're just sitting on our asses doing nothing."

"We're biding our time, that's all. Be patient," Boris said. "The cameras are almost complete."

"You've still been working on that?" Ramona asked.

"Of course I have. We have a plan, right?"

I looked around the room. Did we? We'd talked about it, but it felt like a pipe dream.

"Yeah. We have a plan," Atlas said, but there was uncertainty laced with his words.

"Y'all should have let me go," Cypress argued.

"Punish one, punish all, remember?" I told her.

"You can't put that on me. I want out of here. At some point it's always survival of the fittest."

"Hey now, we can't be thinking like that," Ned protested. "We're in this together. And we're going to get all of us out of here."

The group as a whole seemed more resolved this time, but I was still afraid to get my hopes up again.

# Colin

## Chapter 9

When Lachlan and I rolled up to the airstrip I was fully aware of the stares and surprised faces greeting us. No one protested though.

As we stood around waiting to board, I took a moment to look around.

All of Bravo team had mates and families seeing them off, but for the first time, they weren't the only ones. Michael, Linc, and Tucker did too.

I couldn't watch Linc and Christine as they said their goodbyes without guilt slicing through me once again.

"Promise me you'll come back without a scratch this time," she teased him.

He laughed. "You know better than that, but I'll try."

My shoulders started to sag, but I pushed all the negative feelings aside and turned to focus on Michael instead. His mate, Callie, was one of Lane's deputies and she tended to be a bit of a mother hen to all of us on the team as if adopting two teenage opossum shifters wasn't enough for her.

"We'll be here waiting when you return," she assured him as she wrapped her arms around his neck and brazenly kissed him.

"Mom!" Autumn shrieked. "Cool it. Everyone's watching."

Her parents just chuckled as they finished their intimate moment before he let go of his mate and pulled his daughter into his arms.

"There is nothing gross or embarrassing about telling or showing those you care about just how much you love them."

He kissed the top of her head as she wiggled away from him and wrapped an arm around Callie.

Michael shook hands with his son and then pulled him into an embrace too.

"Kevin, I'm counting on you to keep them safe. You're the man of the house when I'm away."

Callie rolled her eyes, and I hid a grin. We all knew she was badass and more than capable of protecting their little family.

"You can count on me, Pops. Besides, you'll be back before we even have time to miss you."

"I'm counting on that."

Giving them their space, I looked around as Bravo team also said their goodbyes, but something else caught my attention as I turned to Tucker and Annie with a scowl.

"This is total bullshit, and I am sick of it. Are these missions going to suddenly become a regular thing? Because I didn't sign on for this crap. What am I supposed to do while you're off on your little boys' trip all the time? It's not fair."

"I know, but it's necessary."

"No, it's not. Look around, Tucker. There are plenty of much more qualified men going. They don't need you. You'll probably just get in their way anyway."

He sighed as he hugged her.

"I know you're just scared, but it's going to be okay. I'll be home in a few days."

"And then we're going to talk about this."

"I know."

I didn't know how he put up with her. I wanted to smack some sense into her, but knew it was none of my business. Still, the relief on his face when Silas announced it was time to board made my heart hurt.

The one good thing, I supposed, was that I was so disgusted by Annie's final words to my friend and worried about Tucker, that I wasn't focused on my own emotions for once as we loaded up for our next big mission.

We already knew more about this mission than we usually got pre-boarding, but Michael and Silas both went through a full briefing with us anyway.

Each of us were given our own assignments. I wasn't exactly surprised to find myself on perimeter monitoring. They were letting me tag along, but they weren't going to let me anywhere near the action.

I sighed. It was better than nothing. I supposed I was going to have to prove myself all over again until they could trust me again.

It was stupid. I'd done nothing wrong. My emotions hadn't affected my actions, yet I knew that if one of my brothers were going through something similar I'd be concerned about them too.

Keeping my head down and doing my job with no issues or complaints was what I was going to have to do for now. I could live with that.

It was a short flight compared to the last mission I'd gone on and I was grateful for it. I didn't have time to freak out too badly. Lachlan and Tucker had kept up a constant flow of conversation that distracted me too. I suspected that was done on purpose, but I was okay with that, too.

When we landed and unloaded, there was a bus waiting for us that took us to a nearby house. Tarron and Taylor immediately started setting up surveillance.

"I've already cracked into this guy's security system, so we'll have eyes on everyone," he explained.

"Great job," Michael praised as he wandered around overseeing everyone's job without micromanaging them or interfering. That's what made him a great leader.

Meanwhile Silas barked orders.

I didn't have anything on my prep list, so I just stood back out of the way until my room was assigned and I hid in there instead. No surprise, Michael, Lachlan, and Tucker were assigned to the same room. Four large men in a room of two sets of bunks designed for kids wasn't ideal, but I'd stayed in worse.

The afternoon passed by in a whirlwind of activities as we got a good mark on the area. It was decided that going in at night was our best opportunity.

"I've got enough still feed to loop now," Tarron informed us. "Just say when."

"Tucker and I are taking to higher elevations here and here," Ben said, pointing out their designated locations on a large map that was now hanging on the wall.

"I could have used Tucker too," Baine complained.

Tucker took it all in stride as he laughed and held up his hands. "Gentleman, there's plenty of me to go around."

He was always good-natured but there was something freer about him when we were on an away mission. Not that anyone could fault him that. His mate practically had him castrated back home and kept him on a very short leash.

Seeing them together made me question the sanity of anyone willing to take a mate. I sure wasn't in any hurry to find one. Though Michael and Linc made it look easy and all the guys on Bravo team seemed to have great relationships with their mates. Still, just the thought of being saddled down to an Annie made me okay with the idea of being a lifelong bachelor.

"We need to get in and out undetected. Those of you on exterior watch are just precautionary. With any luck we're just going to go with the feed on loop, get them rounded up and out of there," Silas exclaimed.

"We'll be on the plane heading for home before this one even knows we were there," Michael said.

"So we've confirmed the barn is where the witches are stored, but not where the Collector stays, right?" Walker asked.

"Affirmative," Taylor told him.

"Okay, load up and file out," Michael added.

We once again boarded the bus. This time I took a good look at the bus driver. I could have sworn I'd seen that guy before.

When I sat down I asked Lachlan about it.

"Who do we contract to drive us to things like this and how do we keep them silent?"

I wasn't certain I wanted to know the answer to that, but curiosity had me asking anyway.

"You must have missed the memo on that one. Patrick added a new unit to the Force. Foxtrot. They're specifically hired for transportation. All pilots and drivers are now part of that unit instead of risking outsourcing resources. This one was driving us on the last Collector mission too. I never caught his name though. They seem to keep their mouths shut, heads down, and don't get involved much in missions."

"Strictly transportation then?"

"Exactly."

"Cool."

He frowned. "Don't even think about it. We actually need you on Delta so keep your head on straight out there today."

"I wasn't thinking that," I insisted, and it was true.

I couldn't imagine being on any other team. Delta was by far the best and they were my family. If I was kicked off the team, I had no idea what I would do with my life. I knew now wasn't the time to let that thought sink in. No good would come of it.

We were mostly quiet on the drive over.

"Going dark," the driver said as he killed all lights on the bus and put on night vision goggles to drive us across the property.

The drive was uneventful. We never even passed by the main house.

The barn sat off in the field all by itself. There was nothing within sight of it which made our job easy.

"Set your watches. Top of the hour in three, two, now," Silas said as we all synchronized. "Let's go. Ten minutes in and out. No more."

"Eagles, go," Michael said.

Ben and Tucker took off to get in position. Forty-five seconds later they both called in confirmation.

"Perimeter, go," he said.

I ran to get into my position just outside the front door.

"Check," I said as soon as I was in place.

"Extraction team, go," he finally said.

Walker, Painter, Grant, Taylor, and Linc were charged with extractions.

I stood by as Baine stepped in and blew the lock on the front door in a matter of seconds then motioned the team inside.

As the door flew open, my entire body tensed.

I took a deep breath, and a growl escaped me.

Something was very wrong.

My first instinct was to call a retreat, but just as I opened my mouth to call off the extraction team, I heard the last thing I ever expected.

*Mate,* my wolf growled in my head.

My heart raced as I frantically looked around.

Lachlan must have noticed because he shook his head shooting me a look of warning as I began to freak out.

I sniffed the air again.

*Mine,* my wolf alerted me.

"Shit!"

"Colin, no," Lachlan cried over the radio as I took off running into the building.

"Report," Silas demanded.

"Colin left his post. He's inside the building."

"What the hell are you doing?" Michael yelled in my earpiece.

"It's not what you think," I growled.

"We have eight identified," Grant reported.

"They aren't coming easily," Painter added.

"The girl recognizes us. She's alerted the others," Taylor said.

"Shit. She thinks we're the bad guys," Walker explained. "Calm down. We're here to help, to rescue you."

"It's Mirage, right?" Taylor said calmly.

I looked at her and then at the woman she was talking to. She looked terrified as she backed the others into a corner and then they all disappeared right before my eyes.

*Mate*, my wolf howled.

"It's her gift," Walker explained. "Please Mirage. We don't have time for this. We need to go. You can trust us."

He stepped toward where we'd last seen them, but somehow, I knew they had moved. I could smell her so clearly.

When he got too close to her, I jumped in front of him and growled menacingly.

*Mate,* my wolf kept reminding me.

"What the hell, Colin?" Grant yelled.

"Get him the hell out of here," Painter insisted.

Linc stepped forward to physically remove me. He was a tough opponent and had several inches on me, but I had far more to lose.

"You're scaring her," I told them through gritted teeth as I backed up in the opposite corner of the room where I knew without a doubt my mate was holed up.

I didn't need to see her. I could smell her, and I could vividly feel her presence.

"Wait, look," Grant said. "Why are you on that side of the room?"

I growled in response.

"Shit! It's his mate," Taylor said. "You know where she is despite her cloak, don't you?"

I wasn't about to answer that.

"We have incoming. Get the hell out of there," Silas yelled.

"Dammit. Pull out," Painter said.

The others started backing up, but then Painter lunged behind me as if he could somehow grab her and make a run for it.

I let him because I knew she had moved again. Only to protect her, I'd held my ground despite every instinct within me to shield her.

"I've got the door welded back the best I can," Baine said through coms. "Get your asses out of there."

"Please," Taylor tried once more. "We just want to help you and take you away from this place. What you think you saw the other night wasn't what you think. We're the good guys."

She was practically begging, but the cloak never dropped. My mate was still panicking.

"Ninety seconds and you'll be trapped," Michael said a little too calmly. "Get the hell out of there now."

Slowly the extraction team retracted and withdrew from the building.

"What happened?" I heard someone whisper.

"Someone's coming," I told them. "And it's not us. The extraction team was called to pull out."

"Why are you still here?" another voice asked.

"Because I'm not leaving here without her," I said through gritted teeth.

"The Collector," my mate said.

I wasn't even sure how I knew it was her, but I did.

"Back to your rooms. Get in bed and do your best to pretend to sleep. I don't know what alerted him."

I heard footsteps and then suddenly saw them running from the room, all but her. I stayed ready to fight. Someone would have to kill me first, because there was no way I was leaving her here.

My heart raced and we shared a wide-eyed look as the front door opened again, and footsteps echoed down the hallway.

*Hide,* she mouthed, and her eyes cut to the small bathroom in the room.

She was trying to protect me now, but it felt all wrong. I could take this guy down.

"What is going on?" the man yelled out. "Mirage! What are you up to?"

I pulled out the pistol holstered at my hip when he started checking the room and heading my way.

She shook her head almost imperceptibly. If I hadn't been looking right at her, I would have missed it. Still, I was at the ready when he walked into the bathroom and looked around. There was this weird haziness when I looked right at him and raised my gun.

But he turned and walked back out.

"I don't understand why you are doing this. Haven't I been good to you? Well, haven't I?"

"Y-yes, sir," she stuttered.

"Then why?"

"Why what, sir?"

"Why are you using your powers against me?"

"Huh? What do you mean?"

"Just before bed I checked the camera feeds, and do you know what I saw?"

She shook her head.

"I saw light. So I asked myself, what's wrong with the timers? Why haven't the lights gone out? Why isn't everyone in their beds? And then I come here and find everything as normal."

"Shit! Fix the feed now," I whispered in a voice too low for the human's ear.

I had a bad feeling I knew where he was going with this. We hadn't done our due diligence when setting the record loop. We had rushed it and it had cost us the mission.

"I see this," he yells holding up a tablet to show her.

"What am I supposed to see?" she asked.

He turned the device back to him and his forehead wrinkled.

"What is going on here? I know what I saw. This is all you. It has to be. Do you enjoy making a fool out of me? Do you?"

"N-no, sir. Please. I don't know what you're talking about. I've done nothing wrong."

He pulled up what looked like a stylus, and I saw her violently shaking her head.

"I swear. Please. We've done nothing."

"Well, something weird is going on around here and that means one of you are up to something. You know the rules, Mirage."

He pressed down on the pen thing, and she screamed as she dropped to her knees.

I was ready to move in and permanently end the guy. I had no idea what sort of power he had over her, but I was sick to my stomach and feeling more helpless than ever as I stood there watching her shake all over like she was having some sort of epileptic seizure.

The others were screaming from down the hallway too.

Despite it all, her eyes begged me not to intercede.

"Stand down, Colin. We'll proceed with extraction the second this asshole leaves," Michael assured me.

This was worse than watching Linc get shot. It was worse then any nightmare I'd had since.

That was my mate, and it was my job to protect her at all costs.

I stood up ready to move in.

"Don't do it," Michael begged me.

I knew then that they were watching everything.

"He's leaving," he finally said. "We have a new feed in place. Go comfort your mate and let's get them the hell out of there."

He didn't have to tell me twice as I ran to her side and dropped to my knees, pulling her into my arms.

# Mirage

## Chapter 10

Somehow, the pain of it all subsided the moment he touched me.

"Mirage, are you okay?" Atlas yelled out.

"I'm fine. Are you guys okay?"

I forced myself to stand even though my legs were still a bit wobbly. When I swayed, the man gently supported me. The warmth that washed over me was equal parts amazing and terrifying.

"What happened?" Cypress asked.

"I don't know. He thought I was screwing with the camera feed."

The man growled. "That was our fault. We rushed this and didn't know the lights were on a timer. The loop put in place was still lighted."

"Who's that?" Mags asked as seven faces poked through my door.

I sighed. "I don't know. One of them."

"Them? But you said we couldn't trust them."

"I know what I said, Mags."

"But you saved this one, didn't you?" Ned challenged.

"I hid him from the Collector."

"But why? If he'd been caught we'd never have to face punishment like that," Ramona said.

When she took a step towards him, I intercepted and growled at her.

"Did you just growl at her?" Atlas asked. "You never channel your wolf. We've even taken bets on whether you actually have an animal spirit or not."

Gwen eyed us suspiciously but kept uncharacteristically quiet.

"So what do we do with him?" Boris asked.

The guy yelped as he suddenly started floating through the air.

"Put him down, Boris," I hissed through clenched teeth.

"Do as she says," Gwen warned him. "Keep calm, Mirage. We're all just trying to figure this out. He meant no harm."

"Why does she care about him? He's one of them," Ned said, completely oblivious.

*Mate,* a voice in the back of my head growled.

It wasn't the first time. I'd been hearing that word on repeat since just before I laid eyes on the guy.

"He protected us, remember?" Mags said. "At first physically when we moved corners and then by staying there while we relocated again after realizing he was alerting the others to our position, right?"

The guy gave a curt nod.

"But why?" Ned asked again.

I wanted to groan. I'd heard about mates before, I just never dreamed it would happen to me.

He held a hand to his ear and nodded.

"We'll be ready," he said before turning to us. "My team is coming back through. It's time to get you all out of here. No one gets left behind."

"No way," Ned said. "Mirage, you told us not to trust them."

I was torn now. I didn't know what to think.

"I don't trust the wolf collectors," I said as I spat out their name. "What kind of shifter buys witches?"

He sighed and scrubbed his face with his hand and then turned to talk directly to me as if my friends weren't even in the room. His eyes begged me to listen, and I wanted to trust him. It was a bit infuriating. I didn't trust anyone, but I did trust him.

"They were undercover trying to pick up leads on some of the Collectors."

"They bought witches," I argued. "I was there. I know what I saw."

He nodded. "They did. Three of them. They are safe. I promise. You can even see them for yourself soon. But we have to go. And we need to move quickly."

"Do you trust him? Forget the others. You protected him for a reason, Mirage. You've never doubted your instincts before," Ramona reminded me.

Slowly I nodded. "I trust him," I whispered.

"Then let's get the hell out of here."

"Are you sure the Collector is blind right now regarding the cameras?"

"He is," the man said. "My team will blow the lock on the door again in about four minutes. They're en route now."

"Screw that. Let's go," she said.

I laughed at the confused look on his face.

"We're really doing this?" Cypress asked.

"Calm down," Gwen warned.

We all ran to the front door. Before his friends could even return, Ramona grabbed Boris and walked through the front door then returned for Cypress.

"What? You could have left at any time?"

"It's not that easy," I told him. "You said the cameras are down. That's a game changer. You saw what happens when we step out of line. He didn't just shock me, but all of us at once."

He gritted his teeth and reached his hand out to touch my arm like he was grounding himself to me. I didn't understand it, but I knew the feeling. I'd felt it when he made the last remnants of pain disappear with his touch.

"Who is this guy, Mirage?" Atlas demanded.

When he stepped forward, the man pushed me behind him and squared off with him.

"You don't want to do this." The warning was low and guttural.

"And we don't have time for this," Ramona insisted as she grabbed Magnolia and disappeared again.

"Take it down a notch, Atlas."

"Why are we trusting him? We can just leave him here and disappear. We don't need him."

"She does," Gwen whispered. "He's Mirage's true mate."

I gasped at her announcement and my cheeks burned with embarrassment.

When Ramona returned this time, she was grinning. "They have a bus to get us far away from here quickly. Come on. We need to hurry."

She grabbed Ned even while he protested and pulled him through.

"Don't do anything stupid, Atlas. I'm serious about this," Gwen warned him.

"Don't you dare betray us or hurt her," he warned.

"I could never hurt her," the man said.

Atlas held out his hand and then slowly the two men shook hands just as Ramona popped in and grabbed Gwen.

"Are we good here then, because we're kind of in the middle of an escape here."

"Atlas," he told the guy as if I had been cloaked or something and not even here.

"Colin," the man responded, sending my heart pitter-pattering at an even faster rate.

*Colin. My mate's name is Colin.*

There was power in a name and once it was known, it couldn't be unknown. It just made it all the more real.

"This is Mirage," Atlas told him as I shot him a glare over Colin's shoulder.

Colin turned to face me and gave an adorable little half smirk that made my heart melt.

"I know," he whispered and then winked at me.

Ramona chose that moment to reappear and grab me.

I growled at her, but she didn't let go. Everything went black for a second and then I was on the other side. It was chaos as someone grabbed me and ran toward the waiting bus.

"Too cool," one of the men said. "Why the hell didn't you guys escape ages ago."

I groaned. "It's a long story."

Atlas came through next and then, finally, Colin.

I stopped and stared back at him. He was frantically looking for me, so I pushed the man away and ran back to his side.

"I'm fine," I told him.

His body shuddered against mine.

"Come on. I really need to get you the hell away from here before I lose it," he confessed.

One of the men clearly in charge seemed to take a headcount and nod.

"All accounted for this time. Get us the hell out of here."

Then he turned towards us, or rather Colin, with a scowl.

"Not now," my mate told him.

"Colin."

"Not now," he growled, and the man sighed but backed off.

Everyone was quiet on the drive out.

Despite everything, I expected them to take us to a new collection. Instead, we ended up at a house. Everyone piled out of the bus and inside. My friends and I stayed huddled close together and I stayed within arm's reach of Colin.

He walked over to the two men that seemed most likely in charge. One was big and gruff, the other appeared irritated but more patient with my mate.

"We're not staying here. Get on the phone and get us a flight out of here tonight, or we're getting on the bus and driving home."

"Colin, calm down. You're being irrational," the nicer of the two said.

"Being irrational is totally normal for a mating male," Gwen explained.

"Would you stop saying that?" I warned her.

"What? Just smell them. They're all shifters too."

"That's not the point," I said through clenched teeth.

"Ah hell. That's what this is all about?"

"Michael, I told you this was not expected behavior for him. Now it all makes perfect sense," one with an Australian accent said.

"I told you I heard her say mate," another agreed. "Now pay up, you pussies."

"Baine, that's enough," the gruff one who was not Michael said.

I was careful to keep track of as many names as I could.

"Silas?" Michael asked the now scowling one.

"Tarron, call it in. The job's done and there's really no reason I can think of to stay, aside from actually getting some goddamn sleep," he muttered.

"You can sleep on the plane," Colin told him, earning him a look that would have terrified anyone, yet my mate didn't falter in the least.

"I mean it, pay up. You know I called this one," Baine insisted as they all set about packing their things.

Colin looked torn on what to do.

"I need to get my things, but I don't want to leave you and I think you all should stay together."

"Relax. I'll grab your bag. It's not like you unpacked anything anyway," the Aussie told him.

"Thanks, Lachlan."

"Why should we all stay together?" Ned asked. "Are we not safe here?"

"Of course you're safe here," Colin insisted. "It's just that you seem close and I'm sure this is a little scary. I don't blame any of you for not trusting us. We haven't earned that yet."

Cypress shrugged. "I don't know. I mean so far there haven't been any chains, whips, or cages."

"Jesus," Colin muttered under his breath as I shot her a look to shut up.

The woman from the trade show approached us and I instinctually took a step back. The others all huddled in around me, but Colin reached for my hand and laced our fingers together.

"It's okay. I told you, it's not what it seemed. This is Taylor."

"You mean Tayla," I corrected.

"T goes by lots of names when she's undercover, but her real name is Taylor," he explained in a soothing voice. "And this is her mate, Grant."

I shook my head. "No. That guy over there is her mate. His name is Walter. I'm good with names. I know what I'm talking about."

The man grinned at me. "It's Walker actually. We were undercover. She's not my wife but is happily mated to Grant."

I was so confused that I didn't know what to think or believe.

Colin took both my hands in his and faced me.

"Do you trust me?"

Slowly I nodded.

"I don't want to," I admitted.

"It's okay. I can understand and even appreciate that. But you know who I am to you, and you have to know that I could never hurt you. Never. We're with an organization called Westin Force. It's comprised of several special ops teams. There are two units represented here today. We protect and, when necessary, rescue shifters."

"I'm not just a shifter," I blurted out, realizing it was the first time I'd ever confessed to anyone that I was a shifter.

"I know. We rescue witches too," he said softly.

There was something calming about his voice.

As I stared up at him, I took a moment to really look at him. I was certain I'd never seen a more handsome man, not even on the television. I could get lost in his eyes and be perfectly content forever. I suddenly understood the draw of my powers to the Collector and why he kept coming back and insisting on being transported to another time and place that made him happy. Staring into Colin's eyes was the closest I'd ever felt to that kind of peace.

"What are you going to do with us?" Ramona asked.

"We're going to take you home," Colin said. "For us that's San Marco. Westin Pack is the largest wolf shifter pack in the world and very connected and safe. But if any of you actually know where you came from and wish to return home, arrangements can be made."

"And that's it?" Mags asked. "You're just going to let us go, no strings attached."

Colin looked at me, unable to answer that question honestly.

"Besides the whole mating thing with you two," she blurted out.

I blushed again, but he chuckled.

"Aside from that, no strings attached."

"Then you're all fools," Cypress said. "No seriously. You have no idea the assets you're just giving up by letting us go."

"Shut up, Cypress," Atlas warned.

"I'm not a witch, just a fox with a clueless master who got duped into buying me," Ned blurted out.

We all laughed knowing it was true.

"The bus is ready to take us to the airport," Silas said. He didn't appear as angry as previously.

Michael clapped Colin on the back as they led the way out.

"You're doing great," he reassured him.

Lachlan had remained nearby the majority of the time, while the others had given us space to talk with Colin like they understood he was the only one of them we trusted.

"Come on, let's get you guys out of here. My wolf isn't going to calm down until we are far away from here," my mate confessed.

As we drove to a nearby airstrip the eight of us practically had our noses glued to the window. I'd never really seen the world quite like this before and it was fascinating.

No one said much as we arrived and transferred to an airplane.

"It's going to be a little tight in here as we're nearly at capacity," Taylor complained. "If you'll take a seat and buckle up, when we reach altitude and the pilot says it's okay, you can all retreat to the bedroom. I'm sure Colin is happy to continue answering any questions you have. And this is Lachlan. He's our resident psychologist if anyone needs someone to talk to."

"Why aren't we being transported in cages?" Gwen asked.

Taylor growled, and I was starting to think I really had been wrong about her.

"You aren't animals. No more cages, no chains, nothing. You're free now."

"Free?" I whispered.

What did that even mean? I understood it in concept, but I had no idea how to apply it to my life. It was too overwhelming to even think about.

The excitement of our escape was starting to wane, and my body was suddenly heavy with exhaustion. The pressure of takeoff only seemed to compound it further as my eyes began drifting closed.

"Lachlan, can you help explain things to the others? I fear my mate has had enough for one night."

Those were the last words I heard before he wrapped an arm around me and I rested my head on his shoulder without protest. The scent of my mate and the hum of the plane lulled me to sleep.

# Colin

## Chapter 11

"They're a really tight group and will feel safer kept together," Lachlan argued.

"I guess we can put them up in one of the connecting suites?" Michael suggested. "It'll be a little cramped for eight people, but doable."

Linc snorted. "Eight? You mean nine."

He pointed to me, where I sat contentedly with my mate sleeping on me. I didn't even care one bit that she drooled a little in her sleep or that she occasionally let out one loud snore when she changed positions. It was cute.

I shrugged my one free shoulder.

Silas shook his head and scowled. "The last thing we need is an unstable mating male."

"I'm holding up just fine," I argued.

"He's doing surprisingly well all things considered," Lachlan agreed.

"Look, I'm taking my mate home. Get on the phone with Kyle or whoever else you need to get the approvals for it, but she's coming home with me and I have plenty of room for the others as well."

"That's against procedure," Silas argued.

"Screw procedure. This is my mate we're talking about. That circumvents the procedures."

"For her maybe, but not the rest of them."

I growled.

Michael jumped to my defense.

"We'll run it by Patrick and Kyle. We can always put a team on the house until they've been properly vetted and debriefed."

"You'll be assuming liability for that one then," Silas told him.

Michael looked at me and sighed. "I know."

I tried not to let it rile me up as he started making the necessary calls. By the time we landed everything was sorted. Due to the mating thing, I was getting my way, but Delta would be stationed around my house twenty-four seven until further noticed.

"It's okay," Walker argued. "We don't mind."

"We were already planning to be away a few days longer," Tucker agreed. "It's fine."

"But what will Annie say?" I asked, worried about my friend and how his psychotic mate would react to this change of plans.

"Let me worry about her. It's still my job, and she should be happy that I'm at least in territory instead of away."

He was being optimistic. We all knew that no matter how much he tried to defend her, she never made things easy for him.

I had to wonder if that's what my life was soon to look like. Would Mirage try to control me like what Annie did to Tucker?

I shivered at the thought, though as I looked down at the beautiful woman in my arms, it was hard to imagine such a thing. Her entire being radiated happiness back to me.

Then again, was that how it had started for him too? I suddenly wanted to know. I'd heard the story about how she'd tricked him into mating her when they were really just pups still. She'd always had a manipulative side to her, yet Tucker was one of the best men I knew and had to have seen something good in her. Right?

It was confusing me, and I knew I needed to stop stressing over his life and focus on my own. I wasn't going to be duped into mating like that. Besides, Annie hadn't been his true mate. Mirage was definitely mine, though. My wolf was happy to remind me of that every few minutes.

I started to relax a little when the plane finally touched down and the door opened, giving me a whiff of home. I didn't mind going on the occasional away mission, but I would never want to do it all the time the way Bravo team did. I was much more of a homebody than I liked to admit, and the smells of Westin brought me comfort.

The others had come out of the room for our descent, but now there was uncertainty and confusion. I didn't think they really believed us when we told them they were free now. Maybe they shouldn't. Until we were confident that they posed no threat to the Pack they would be closely watched, but it wasn't the same as being stuck in captivity.

I remembered the room where Mirage had lived. In truth it was a nice place. I could see where the Lodge would have felt similar to that place, but they weren't going there. They were coming home with me, a real house.

"You're sure about this?" Michael asked me as I lifted Mirage into my arms and carried her off the plane. She didn't even budge.

"I'm positive. We're going home. I only have room for three more in my car though, so someone will have to drive the other four up the mountain."

"No way, we're not splitting up," Atlas insisted.

"Trust me, I understand. If there was any way, I'd do it. It's only about a twenty-minute drive. Four with me and four with…"

"Me," Walker said.

"Not him," Atlas insisted.

I groaned in frustration. "I thought we already cleared that all up. Walker is a friend. All of you will be staying with me because I am not about to let Mirage out of my sight, and I know you all understand why. I get you're a package deal for now, but my car simply doesn't have enough seats."

"Hey man, how about I follow you in your car and you take mine? It seats eight, but if you don't mind being a little cramped for the ride, then it'll work," Ben said. "I just need to take the car seats out first."

He was already heading to his large Suburban before I could even start to protest.

"It's all good. This will be fine," Walker assured me.

"Thanks, man."

Mirage stirred a bit in my arms and wrapped her arms around me, snuggling closer.

"She's really tired," Mags said.

"And she feels safe with you. She never sleeps this hard without being medicated," Gwen explained.

I cringed at the thought of anyone medicating her like that, but I kept it to myself.

We all piled into the big SUV and Ben and I exchanged keys for the rides up.

"Thanks for keeping us together, Colin. It really does mean a lot to us," Atlas said.

"I really hate to ask this of you, but can you hold her while I drive," I surprised us both by saying.

"Yeah, absolutely. Boris, switch places with me so I can sit up front. We don't need him losing his shit with her out of sight right now."

The other man didn't hesitate to make the change, and soon we were off and driving home.

I didn't have to see our surroundings to know the second I officially crossed into Westin Pack territory. A sense of calm washed over me and I knew everything was going to be okay.

We'd been attacked by a Collector in territory before, but we wouldn't be caught off-guard like that again. I was on the team to personally ensure that, strengthening our borders. Now that job was even more important to me.

I pulled up to my house and put the car in park.

"We're here. Hold on and I'll come around to get her," I told Atlas as the others slowly exited the car.

Ben pulled up next to me and got to work putting the car seats for his triplets back into his vehicle and tossed me my keys.

"Left yours in the ignition."

"Thanks. Go on and get them settled. It's really late and the sun will be rising soon. I think everyone could use a good night's sleep."

"Yeah. I think you're right."

"And Colin?"

"Yeah?"

"Congrats on finding your mate."

"My mate," I said solemnly and then barked out a laugh. "That's going to take some getting used to."

Even though I knew my house was unlocked, the others all congregated on the stairs looking uncertain of what to do.

I gathered Mirage up into my arms, but this time she stirred a little more on the transfer. I froze, not wanting to wake her. She sniffed me and then sighed contentedly and settled back down. I couldn't help but grin down at her.

"Door's open, head on in," I told them just as Walker and Tucker pulled up. "It's okay. Just make yourself at home."

Hesitantly they did as I told them.

"Did you two draw the short straw or something?" I asked the guys.

"Or something," Walker said.

"Annie's not expecting me tonight so instead of waking her I asked to go ahead and take a turn."

"And Lachlan wanted to be here in case anyone needed him, but I feel like everyone's so tired that he'll be better off helping them in the morning after a good night's sleep," Walker explained.

"Thanks for doing this, really," I told them.

"Tarron's going to swing by tonight and set up some surveillance cameras just as a precaution and only around the perimeter of your house. No one will even know they're there. He'll put in a few motion sensors too and while local wildlife could trigger them, it's still preferable to sitting up all night over the next few days while we get them acclimated."

"Sounds like a plan. Thanks, but I'm going to ditch you both and go put my woman to bed now."

Leaving them to it, I walked inside. The rest of the gang was all standing around in shock.

I sighed. "I know. It's ridiculous and way too much for just one man, but it was my grandparents' house and when they passed it came to me. I grew up here. The place was already furnished so I've only made a few changes, but that means there are five extra bedrooms. Four of them are upstairs and one more on this level. My room is also on this level. Mirage is staying with me. I can't explain it and she may freak out when she wakes up in the morning, but I need her close to me."

"It's okay," Gwen assured me and then turned to the others. "I promise he won't hurt her."

"Let me get her settled and then I'll give you guys a quick tour of the place."

Before anyone could protest, I headed down the hall to my room. I pulled the covers back while juggling her with one hand and carefully laid her in my bed. The sight of her there affected me in ways I couldn't even explain. Plus, it just felt right.

*Mine,* my wolf sighed happily.

"Mine," I whispered in agreement.

Before I could let myself freak out about it, I walked back to the others waiting for me. It dawned on me then that they had nothing but the clothes on their backs.

I cringed. "I'm sorry. I don't have a lot of clothes and things here, but we can work on that first thing in the morning. Are you okay for the night? Does anyone need anything?"

"We're fine," Boris assured me. "Just show us to our cages."

I scowled. "There will be no more cages. I thought we explained that."

Still, they all looked skeptical.

"I'm much too tired for this right now. I'm sure you can all use a good night's sleep too. You're just going to have to trust me that you are safe here tonight. We'll go over the rest tomorrow. So, this is the living room, dining room, and kitchen. I'm not much of a cook, but feel free to help yourselves to anything. I'll make a grocery run tomorrow as well so think about what you want and we'll start a list in the morning." I turned to the left and opened the door at the end of the hall. "This is the garage." I closed that and opened another door. "And this leads to the basement. There's a full gym down there if anyone wants to work out. The big TV, video games, and bar are all down there too."

They looked like they were either in shock or caving to exhaustion. I wasn't sure which, so I sped things up and turned toward the other end of the house.

"My room is at the end of the hall. That's where Mirage is now. Bathroom to the right, another bedroom to the left. There's a desk in there that I do use as a home office at times, so it may be a little a messy, but there's a comfortable bed there too. Come on," I said, leading them all upstairs. "Up here is pretty simple. This is a sitting room area to hang out in or whatever. I rarely come here, but my cleaning lady keeps it tidy so everything should be in order. Four bedrooms, each with its own bath. That one has a king bed, queen bed, two sets of bunkbeds, and the last one there has a daybed with a trundle that pulls out for an extra bed. So really, I guess there are plenty of beds up here for everyone if you don't mind sharing rooms, or there are lots of couches, whatever you prefer."

I turned to leave, but they just stood there staring at me.

"Um, where are we supposed to sleep?" Cypress asked.

I groaned. "I'm really exhausted you guys, so please, just work with me here. I just told you there are four bedrooms up here." I walked over and opened the door to the king room to show them and then ran around and opened all the other doors too. "Take your pick and find a bed."

They shared a confused look.

"We've never had a master that just let us sleep wherever we want," Ramona said sadly.

"I'm not your master. You are not my collection or my property. You are my guests here."

"I'll handle it," Atlas finally said. "Mags, you take the room with the biggest bed."

She shook her head. "It's too much for one person."

"I'll stay with her," Gwen offered.

"Okay. So Ramona and Cypress, you can either stay in the smaller bedroom or the one with the pull-out thingy he mentioned, or you can each have your own room."

Cypress shook her head.

Ramona rolled her eyes.

"Come on, Cypress. We'll take this one," she said dragging the distraught girl to the queen room.

"Okay boys, we're going to take the bunk room."

Five rooms and they consolidated down to only three. I shook my head but didn't argue.

"I'll see you all in the morning."

"Aren't you going to lock us in for the night?" Atlas asked.

"No, I'm not. If you require a lock for your personal safety, there's one on each door. Just press the middle button in."

"But won't we still be able to get out?" he questioned.

"Atlas, that's the point. You're free to roam around the house all you want. In a few days you should be able to leave on your own with no issues, but there is a debriefing and acclimation period, so until that's over, you'll be here with me, okay?"

Tears sprang to his eyes. "Okay," he said softly, like he was still not quite sure he believed it but was beginning to let a little hope in.

"You remember how to get back to my room?"

He nodded. "Yes, sir."

"If you need anything at all, that's where you can find me."

I was anxious to return to my mate.

When I did, I found she hadn't moved at all. I couldn't even fathom just how exhausted she must be. Not wanting to freak her out, I left my clothes on and stayed above the covers as I laid next to her in bed. Her scent was already filling my room, and I knew there was nothing in this world that would ever smell better to me than my mate.

Julie Trettel

# Mirage

## Chapter 12

I stretched feeling more rested than I could ever remember. The sheets were so soft around me that I felt as though I were floating on a cloud. And the smell surrounding me was comforting and familiar even though I couldn't quite place it in my half-conscious state.

"Mmm," I moaned in pleasure. "So nice."

"Good morning," a strange voice said, waking me fully as my eyes flew open.

This wasn't my room. And that wasn't my Collector's voice. Where was I?

The weight on the bed shifted next to me and I looked over to find a strange man lying there. I screamed and scrambled up to the top of the bed as I balled myself up as small as possible along the headboard.

Where was I?

How did I get here?

What had happened?

I started to take a mental assessment of my body. I'd seen and heard of things, horrendous things.

Had he drugged me?

96

I couldn't recall much in my panicked state.

He jumped out of bed and threw his hands in the air.

"Mirage, calm down. It's me, Colin."

"Colin?" I whispered as my eyes widened and everything came crashing down on me.

Westin Force.

The extraction.

My mate.

I gulped hard.

I had a mate, a true mate. He'd swooped in like a knight in shining armor and rescued me and my friends.

I looked around. Where were they?

"Where am I? Where are my friends?"

"Relax. You're safe. You all are. This is my home. Our home, I suppose," he started to ramble and then stopped and smiled at me.

His hair was disheveled, and he had day-old scruff on his face.

God he was beautiful. I could stare at him all day, but something was nagging me in the back of my mind.

"They're all sleeping upstairs. Trust me, you're safe here. There's no way for anyone to know where you are."

My whole world came crashing in around me.

"Shit! You're wrong. I have to get the others and keep moving before he finds us."

"Didn't you just hear a thing I said? Mirage, you're safe. You're free now."

I shook my head sadly. "I'll never be free, Colin. And we aren't safe. He'll find us. We need to stay ahead of him."

"What are you talking about?"

"We're his most prized possessions. Don't you get it? He'll stop at nothing to recover us."

"I'll never let that happen. And there is no way he'll ever find you here."

I jumped out of his bed and started pacing.

"You're wrong. All he has to do is track us."

I pulled the sleeve of my shirt up and pointed to the scar just at the edge of my armpit there on the back of my arm.

Colin looked like he was going to be sick.

"He put a tracker on you?"

I nodded. "All of us have one. Along with a device attached directly to our spines for punishment and control. You saw him use it. Fortunately, I know he can only use that in close proximity to us. He did a demo at the trade show where I saw your friends. When I came back and asked the others, they hadn't felt a thing, so that's one positive in all this I suppose."

"Shit. I have to call this in right now. He's a few hours ahead of us thanks to the time zone differences. I'm sure he already knows you're gone. I'll put it on speaker in case Michael needs to talk to you. The bathroom's right there if you need it."

I hesitated but really needed to relieve myself. I left the door slightly cracked to ensure I could easily hear his conversation.

"Michael, we have a problem."

The man yawned. "Can't this wait? It's really early."

"Afraid not. I need a plane gassed and ready within the hour."

"Excuse me?"

"We really botched this one this time. I'm so sorry."

"What happened? Walker and Tucker didn't call anything in. Are they okay?"

"I'm sure they're fine. But we should have checked them closer. Michael, he has trackers on each of them. By now, he knows they're here. Our only option is to keep ahead of him and on the move until we can safely remove the devices when we are as far away from Westin as possible."

"It needs to look like this was just a random stop along the way," he added.

"Exactly. And we don't have much time to make this plausible or else we're going to be leading that sadistic asshole right to my front door."

"And Kelsey. Shit. Let me link Patrick and Kyle in immediately."

As I was finishing up and went out to face him once more, I started pacing.

"Come here," he said, pulling me into his arms. "Your wolf is agitated. I can calm her."

I snorted. "You talk like she's a real being with feelings."

"Isn't she?"

I shrugged. "I've never met her. How would I know?"

He frowned. "You've never set your wolf free?"

Shaking my head, I tried to explain. "I know what I am, but it's never been safe for me to shift before. Sure, I've wanted to, but I couldn't risk it. My current Collector doesn't even know about shifters. That's how they suckered him into paying a premium for Ned and he's not even a witch, just a fox shifter."

"What's going on?" a man asked. "You're all home safe and sound, right? I was told the extraction went well and our guests are crashing at Colin's place."

"Sorry, Kyle. I know that was all a last second change. A very premature last second change that I fear is going to bring hell right to our borders," Michael said before quickly explaining our situation.

"Bloody hell," another said. He had a strong accent I couldn't quite place but reminded me a bit of an old Collector I'd once had.

I shivered at the thought. That hadn't been a good place or time in my life.

"I'm so sorry, Patrick. This is all my fault."

"How the feck is this your fault, Colin?"

He gulped and looked down at me as I stood there in his arms.

"One of the witches we rescued is my true mate. We returned early because I was struggling knowing she was in danger, and all I've done is put the rest of you at risk. I'm so sorry. That wasn't intentional. I had no idea he would go to such extremes as having locator devices installed into them."

"None of us considered this possibility. It's not your fault," Michael said. "Silas and I will take full blame for this one. The entire mission was a mess, and this wasn't our only screw up. We'll fill you both in during debriefing, but Colin's right in that we have to get them in the air and on the move quickly."

"Bravo team will handle it. I'm going to need Delta here, on the ground, and ready. Just in case," Patrick said.

Colin was already shaking his head.

"Didn't you hear me? This is my mate I'm talking about. She's in danger. I know my job, but you can't ask me to just stay behind. Besides, he'll follow them when he sees we've moved on."

There was a moment of silence on the line.

"Okay. Michael, you and Silas work out a combined team to ensure we have full coverage here and away," Kyle conceded. "No good will come from forcing a mating separation right now. Colin needs to stay with his mate."

"Lachlan should go too. Pull the rest from Bravo. I'll call Charlie and Echo home right away. Foxtrot will be waiting for extraction at the airport within the hour," Patrick said before they all said goodbye and hung up.

I looked up at Colin. "I'm scared," I admitted.

In all my life, I'd never once confessed those words to anyone, no matter how bad things had gotten.

"I know. But it's going to be okay. I can fix this."

I sure hoped he was right.

Together we ran upstairs and woke the others to explain what was happening. I learned quickly that when my mate set his mind to something he had laser sharp focus.

He grabbed a duffel bag that was already packed and ready, then hesitated and went back to stuff a few extra things in it.

"We'll have to get clothes and things for everyone at the next stop."

"Where are we going?"

"No idea. For now, it's probably best to keep it that way. Come on."

While we had all gotten ready, it seemed he forgot to notify his team. As we stepped outside, Lachlan was just pulling up and the other two already there looked tired and confused.

"What's going on?" Walker asked.

I still wasn't sure I could trust that guy.

"Trackers. We've got to get them back to the airport and far away from here."

"What?" Tucker asked. "You're serious?"

"I'm sorry I didn't think about it before," I said. "I think I was just in shock."

"It's not your fault, Mirage," Gwen assured me.

"Yeah, none of us even remembered it. We're lucky you did," Ned added.

"I hardly even notice it anymore. Besides we just wanted out of there," Atlas admitted.

"What's going to happen to us now?" Cypress asked.

"Nothing is going to happen to any of you," Lachlan assured us. "We're just going to all go on a bit of a walkabout—or fly-about, I suppose—to hopefully keep him away from here. Once we've plotted enough locations to thoroughly confuse him, we'll head off to the whoop-whoop and have those things removed, yeah?"

"The whoop-whoop?" I asked.

Colin chuckled. "Middle of nowhere. He mostly speaks American English, but every now and then his Australian comes out strong."

"Mostly when he's tired," Walker teased.

"Whatever. Let's go. Half with Colin, half with me. No arguments."

No one complained as we all piled into the two vehicles, and they drove us down the mountain to a small airstrip.

Nothing looked familiar to me. I was certain I'd never seen this place before.

"How hard was I out last night?" I mumbled.

"You were like the sleeping dead," Atlas teased. "As long as you were in lover boy's arms. And he wasn't about to let you out of his reach, except whenever absolutely necessary, like to drive."

I looked up at Colin. "Really?"

He shrugged and smiled, not even bothering to deny it.

A bunch of the Westin Force guys were there and waiting when we arrived.

"I'm really sorry about this. I was so thrown off by the lighting botch up that I didn't even think to scan them," Tarron confessed. "Not my best work."

"It's okay. We can fix this," Colin said with certainty.

I wished I could be as confident as him.

As if sensing my unease, he wrapped an arm around me and pressed his lips to the side of my head. It was an odd sensation, but comforting. I'd never allowed anyone close to me before, not physically. I knew what bad things could come from it, yet his touch didn't feel like I thought it would.

It felt nice.

"We've got this," he whispered.

"Okay, so head on in. They're finishing up final checks now. We're sticking to small places to help blend our true location here better. Grant and Taylor will be traveling with you. Good luck," Silas said holding out his hand to Colin who took it and shook it.

"Thanks, Silas."

"Godspeed."

The rest of us loaded onto the plane and were soon taking off again.

"What's going to happen to us now?" Ramona asked.

"Just a minor detour," Colin insisted. "Let's go see a bit of the world and when it's safe, we'll return here and try again."

He made it sound so simple. Was this really his normal life? Call up a plane and galivant around the world on a whim? Who was this guy?

It was clear that there was a lot I still needed to know about my mate.

"Who's hungry?" Colin finally asked.

# Colin

## Chapter 13

We were in flight for several hours. It gave me time to talk with each of them and get to know them a little better.

Gwen could control the emotions of others. In this instance she'd been invaluable to us all by keeping everyone levelheaded and not freaking out with our change of plans.

Ned truly didn't have any powers. He was just a fox shifter, but he provided much needed comic relief amidst tense moments.

I learned Cypress and Magnolia could both grow things. They weren't the same but similar in their powers. I got a kick out of hearing all about the escape plan they'd concocted before our arrival and what their roles in that would have been.

Boris was old and wise. He had the power of telekinesis. While he was hesitant to use his powers in front of me, I found his the most fascinating. Several of the guys back at headquarters were going to lose their shit when they met him.

While Atlas was an unmated male, I'd learned he was a bear, not a wolf and that provided a little more comfort to me. He acted more like a big brother to my mate and for some reason, my wolf and I were okay with that. He had quickly become an ally to me, a very strong one, when the others still showed fear.

I had already gotten an up-close look at Ramona's powers during the escape. She was still hesitant and skeptical of me though. I couldn't really blame her for that, or any of them really. This couldn't be easy for them. I knew from the few stories they had shared that most of them had been held in captivity in various collections for years. It was all they knew and that broke my heart.

And then there was Mirage, my mate. I grinned like an idiot every time I thought about her, or looked at her, or talked to her. Atlas had pointed it out on more than one occasion. Just her presence shone light through the darkness in my life.

"I'm not really an empath. I can just control other people's emotions, but that also requires a heightened level of empathy to know what emotions need to be controlled. I don't particularly like to just influence people for no reason. And well, you just seem a bit off all of a sudden."

"I'm fine," I told her, but Lachlan was paying close attention to the conversation. "Can we talk?" I asked him when I caught his eye.

"Now? We're about to land."

"Now," I told him. I needed to share this revelation with him. I wanted his opinion. I didn't know what to do about it.

"Now?" Mirage asked.

"It's important," I told her, hoping she'd understand. "We'll just be in the bedroom."

Grant shot me a concerning look.

"Go," Taylor told us.

*Thanks*, I mouthed to her as I got up to leave.

I reached over and gave Mirage's hand a little squeeze.

"This won't take long," I tried to assure her before quickly getting up and walking to the back of the plane. Fortunately, Lachlan followed.

Once safely in the room, he turned on the dampener we kept in there and then buckled into one of the seats.

"You should sit. We really will be landing soon."

I shook my head and began to pace the room as everything bubbled out of me. I told him about the new revelation I'd had regarding me believing my life was of less importance to anyone else on the team because I didn't have a family or anyone waiting on me to return.

I told him all about how that had affected me when Linc pushed me out of the way and took a bullet on my behalf.

The darkness, the depression, the guilt, it all came flowing out of me until I was exhausted and spent with unexpected emotions. And then I told him about how that needed to change now because I did have strings now too. I had a mate.

Lachlan just sat there and listened, then he looked at his watch and scowled.

"Colin, this is a phenomenal breakthrough for you, but if you want to start with self-protection, you might want to buckle in. We will be wheels down any second."

"Shit!" I took the seat next to him and strapped in.

"You're doing great. This level of self-awareness far exceeds my expectations. And honestly, Colin, I think you're going to be just fine. Focus on your new mate right now. Because you're right, you do have a lot to live for now. And I won't belittle your feelings by reminding you that you always did."

I rolled my eyes and groaned.

"Didn't you just?"

"I don't know what you're talking about," he insisted.

I just shook my head.

The second our wheels touched down, I was out of my seat and walking out of the room to check on my mate.

Focus on her?

Oh yeah, I could definitely do that.

A couple of them were crowded around the small windows straining to see where we had landed.

"What is this place?"

"Aruba," Mirage whispered turning an odd shade of green.

"St. Thomas actually," Taylor explained. "What's in Aruba?"

Mirage had a distant look in her eyes when she spoke. "It's our Collector's favorite place in the world. He makes me show him it nearly every day."

"Show him?" Lachlan asked.

She nodded and then suddenly we weren't on the plane anymore. We were instead standing on a beach with crystal clear water before us. And then in the blink of an eye it was all gone, and we were back on the plane.

"Woah," Lachlan said. "It felt like we were really there standing on the beach looking out over the water."

Taylor gripped Grant's arm. "I don't think that's something I could ever get used to."

"Amazing," I whispered.

I remembered how she had hidden them all from us when we came in to rescue them. If she hadn't been my true mate, I wouldn't have sensed her presence or even known she was there. My brain was going a mile a minute with all the ways someone could manipulate her.

My wolf aggressively stirred, wanting to protect her from my thoughts and any future scenarios of someone using her for their own means.

"Um, Mirage, could you please just wrap your arms around him?" Taylor asked.

"What?"

"I don't know what he was thinking, but whatever it was has his wolf really on edge right now and we don't want him wolfing out here. Please. It will calm his inner-wolf."

"Seriously?" Atlas asked.

"Seriously," she assured him.

"Is that like a wolf thing?"

"Not really. Though wolves do crave touch more than other species. From what I've observed, mating in general causes all males to go a little crazy at times and his female's touch is about the only thing that will truly calm him once he's worked himself up like this," Grant explained.

"I'm fine," I lied through clenched teeth, trying to get a grip on my emotions while still considering every possible way Mirage could be manipulated by others.

She hesitantly stepped closer to me and then wrapped her arms around my waist.

The feeling of peace her touch brought was instantaneous as I sighed and crushed her to me.

"Wow. That's crazy. You said all true mates act this way?" Ramona asked.

"Oh, this is nothing," Taylor said with a laugh.

"And you know a lot of different shifter species?" Cypress asked, hopefully.

"We do," she assured her. "While Colin's unit, Delta, is comprised of all canines, Grant and I are on Bravo team and there's only one other wolf in our unit."

"So what are the others?" Gwen asked, curiously.

"Let's see, we have a couple of gorillas, a bear, a fox, and a human," she explained.

"A human?" Boris spat in disgust.

Grant shot his mate an uncomfortable look.

"Yes, you heard me," she stubbornly said. "He's the best of the best."

"But he's human. Human's abuse our kind."

Taylor growled. "Not all of them."

Her protective nature over Jake was evident, and no one said another word.

The pilot and copilot stepped out and then opened the door for us.

"Well, what are you waiting for? This place is paradise," the pilot said with a grin.

Grant and Taylor led the way while I let the others exit the plane ahead of me. I was grateful that Mirage held back and stayed by my side.

"Thanks for doing this. I know it was really last minute," I told the pilot.

"Are you kidding? This is the best assignment I've had since joining Westin Force."

"You're on the new team, Foxtrot, right?"

"Yup, that's us. I'm Beckett and this is Grey."

I held out my hand and shook each of theirs in turn.

"Colin. I'm on Delta. This is my mate, Mirage."

She blushed furiously but managed a little wave.

"Having full reign of our route, means we get to go to all of our favorite places," Beckett said, nudging Grey.

"And the Force is paying for it all. It's like a giant vacation. We were just told to not stay more than two days in any one location. Archie has a team trying to track our follower to help direct us a bit," Grey explained.

"So, whose favorite island is this?" I asked.

"Guilty," Grey said. "Come on. You're going to love it here."

Arrangements had already been made to put us all up in a large house right on the beach. But before we arrived there, I talked to the truck driver about picking up a few things.

"We need some clothes, swimsuits, some personal items, and probably some food."

"The house is already stocked. Silas made sure of it," Grant explained.

"Okay, well they still need clothes and swimsuits, toothbrushes, and stuff like that."

"Okay, okay. I got you," the driver insisted.

We were ushered into the back of a pickup that had been outfitted with benches to chauffeur tourists around instead of a traditional truck bed. There was even an awning shading us above.

We all piled in and he took off for a small local town instead of the big tourist areas.

He parked and jumped out excitedly.

"All you need, here," he insisted.

Much of the area was severely run down and I wasn't confident in our selections, but I didn't want to hurt his feelings. Inside there were rows and rows of colorful dresses and shirts along with a full selection of swimsuits. The toiletries were a bit lacking, but they at least covered our basic needs, and I knew we could always pick up more on our next stop.

"Please, pick out what you need," I told the others. Taylor was great with assisting the women while Lachlan and Grant helped the guys.

I stood back and just watched.

"I told you, all you need."

"You were right."

I learned that it was a storage place for tourism.

"Everything you get there at a bargain. You deal," he told me.

I grinned. "You're sure?"

"Oh yes. Come."

He led me over to a woman watching us closely. Her eyes widened as things began piling up for purchase.

"One thousand American dollars," she finally exclaimed.

Truth be told, it probably would have cost me more had we been on the tourist strip. But our driver discreetly shook his head and frowned.

"Five hundred," I told her.

She started ranting so fast that I could barely understand. I looked to the driver for help.

He grinned and gave me a thumbs up.

When she finally took a deep breath and glared at me she said, "Seven hundred American dollars."

I looked to the driver as he subtly shook his head.

"Six hundred," I countered.

"Done," she said without hesitation.

I paid and thanked her as we loaded up the items and walked back to the truck.

"And that is how things are done in my country," he told me slyly as I helped Mirage into the back.

"Did you really just haggle the prices?" Lachlan asked.

I shrugged. "He told me to do it. Saved us four hundred dollars."

He laughed and shook his head. "It's good to see you relaxed despite everything going on."

Relaxed? I looked at him like he was crazy. I felt anything but relaxed. Until that tracker was out of my mate and we were safely back home, I wouldn't be fully relaxed. Yet, I had to admit, there was something soothing about the island with its luscious green forested mountains and gorgeous views of the Caribbean all around.

Despite the great deal of poverty-stricken areas we passed, the house we pulled up to was nothing short of amazing and the views were spectacular.

I jumped out of the back of the truck when he parked and just stood there staring out into the blue-green water.

"It's beautiful, isn't it?" Taylor said almost reverently.

"Incredible," I admitted.

Grant handled thanking the driver and tipping him while I gave a short wave and led the others inside. With Beckett and Grey there were fourteen of us in total, but the six-bedroom mansion Silas had set us up in had more than enough room for everyone.

Taylor got to work immediately on security while on the phone with Tarron.

The rest of us got busy settling in.

Mirage stood at the window staring out at the sea with longing.

I walked up behind her. "It's beautiful, isn't it?"

She jumped and then immediately relaxed.

"I've never seen anything like it before, not in real life. Only in pictures," she said softly.

"Can we go swimming in the pool?" Gwen asked, interrupting our moment.

"Can I go to the beach? I've never felt sand before," Magnolia admitted.

"It's too bright here," Boris complained.

For those that had been in captivity for many years, I would imagine the sun would seem far brighter. It was a good thing Lachlan had thought to grab sunglasses and plenty of sunscreen for each of them.

"Relax," he told them. "You'll need to change into your new swimsuits and put plenty of sunscreen on. You've been indoors a long time and the Caribbean sun can be brutal for anyone."

"Wait, you're really going to let us have some time out there?" Mirage asked.

I sighed. "You aren't prisoners anymore. You're free to do as you please and go where you want. We're only trying to keep you safe until we can remove those tracking chips. Then you will be truly free."

# Mirage

## Chapter 14

I heard what he was saying. They were pretty words, but I didn't fully understand them.

Free? What did that even mean?

I lifted my face towards the sun, squinting up at its brightness. Even through the window I could feel the heat as I stood there relishing in the feel of its splendor.

My memories of the blue sky and bright sun didn't do justice to this moment.

Still, the travel and emotions of the day were weighing heavily on me, and I was exhausted.

The others excitedly ran around checking out the house. It was much like I imagined our Collector lived in, extravagant and over-the-top, yet there was a peace to it too. The bright colors adorning the walls invited a sense of calm. I liked it here immensely, but I also knew this wasn't my life and this was never going to be my home. Just like any other transport hub, this was nothing more than a stop along the way to a new unknown destination.

"Where should we change?" Cypress asked solemnly.

I cringed at her words. Most Collectors were civil enough and gave us some privacy at least. But others insisted on inspecting their purchases from head to toe. It was humiliating and I always feared one would try to touch me when that happened.

Shaking my head, I refused to think about it.

"There are plenty of rooms and bathrooms in this place," Lachlan told them. "Just find a place you're comfortable enough to change."

The others all stopped and turned to stare at him like he had two heads. I understood that, but it was clear he did not.

In the end we did as we were told and then dumped all of our things in a pile in the living room. The couches in there looked so comfy and I wanted to just lay down and see if it was as warm and cozy as it looked, but I didn't dare.

None of us knew these people well enough yet to understand what would set them off. It was always something. Ned's refusal to shift. Or one of my former Collector's freaked out if everyone didn't stand and bow to him when he made his walk-through.

It was only a matter of time before we saw their ticks too. I was worried for when that would happen with so many of them watching over us. Things could get ugly fast, and I was going to need to be ready when that happened.

For all their smooth words, I didn't believe any of it. Yet, there was something about Colin that made me long for them to be true. I trusted him, and that terrified me because he'd given me no real reason to trust him, but also no reason not to.

Taylor had disappeared while on the phone and when she returned something transpired silently between her, Grant, and Colin. But she turned to us with a smile.

"Who wants to go to the beach?" she asked.

"Really?" Mags squealed.

"Absolutely. You're welcome to go on your own. We really do mean it when we say you are free here. We aren't Collectors and you are no longer in captivity, but I also see the skeptical looks on your faces. If it makes you more comfortable, Lachlan is happy to escort those of you who would like to go to the beach."

"There's also the pool," Grant added. "Or television, a nap even. It's up to you."

I looked around at the others and we all turned to Atlas for help.

"We'll go to the beach," he told them. "Lachlan can come along."

It was kind of pathetic that we all nodded in agreement. Hearing you can go by yourself and wanting to take them up on that were two different things. The world out there was scary. I didn't know how it operated. Was it even safe?

At least with Lachlan, someone was watching out for us.

"Are you coming too?" I asked Colin.

He looked towards Taylor but she shook her head.

"I need to deal with a few things here first and then I'll try to meet you down there."

He reached out and touched my arm, and my whole body leaned into him. It was weird, yet it didn't scare me.

He made me feel safe, like everything was going to be okay.

"Mirage, come on," Gwen said practically squealing with excitement.

I looked into Colin's eyes in a way that should have been uncomfortable for the both of us, but he just smiled and nodded encouragingly until I turned and followed my friends outside.

Gwen couldn't help herself. She ran over to the pool and dipped her toe into the water.

Cypress gasped and turned to watch for Lachlan's reaction.

He was just grinning. "Go ahead and jump in if you'd like. Wait, can you swim?"

"I can," Gwen admitted. "I'm a sea lion shifter."

I gasped. I'd never heard her confess her animal spirit like that before. From the looks on everyone else's faces, they didn't know that about her either.

Her eyes widened with unanswered questions.

Lachlan jogged back into the house for a minute.

"Do it, before he comes back," Ned challenged.

She looked at the pool and then back at him. I knew the moment her chin defiantly jutted out that she was going for it. I just hoped we didn't get in trouble for it.

Gwen turned back to the pool and dove in headfirst.

Ramona gasped as her hands flew to her mouth.

The rest of us ran to the edge of the pool just as Gwen surfaced and squealed with excitement.

"It's amazing."

Lachlan returned and we were all silenced at once.

"Relax," he said. "I was just double checking with Taylor. This place is secure. You're all free to shift if you'd like."

My jaw dropped.

Shift?

I gulped hard.

I'd never done that before. I wasn't even sure I knew how.

"For real?" Gwen asked.

"Yes, but only up here and not on the beach, just in case. We can't control people walking or riding horseback along the beach or boats visible from the shore, but here around the house is fine."

Gwen started to sob. "You're sure?"

"I wouldn't lie to you," he assured her.

The next thing I knew, Gwen was taking off her bathing suit and tossing it up on the side of the pool, and then suddenly, she wasn't Gwen anymore. I mean, she was, but not in her human form. She was large and golden brown, splashing and flipping through the water. Occasionally she'd surface and bark out in pure joy.

I wasn't sure how I knew she was so happy, but I was certain of it.

Next Boris shifted and a weasel looking creature scurried about.

"What is he?" I asked Atlas.

Ramona rolled her eyes. "He's a sable."

"What's that?"

116

She groaned this time. "It's a sort of weasel out of Asia. He's cute."

Atlas nearly choked as he tried not to laugh. "Yeah, cute," he said sarcastically.

"Whatever." She glared at him.

"He really is cute," I said. "I've never heard of his kind before."

Atlas shrugged. "They're probably near extinction."

"Actually, his kind is very plentiful, just more region specific so it's not common to find one outside of Asia," Lachlan corrected.

"Well, before you freak out, I'm a Pyrenean desman and we are in fear of extinction," Ramona explained. "My tribe was discussing repopulation efforts before my capture."

"So basically, your Collector had no idea what sort of treasure he was harboring, huh?" Lachlan asked.

"He was an idiot," Ramona assured him before shifting into the oddest-looking creature I'd ever seen. Never in my life would I have dreamed that the beautiful Ramona would turn into such an ugly creature.

As she scurried past me, I yelped and jumped back. It didn't slow her a bit though as she dove into the water to splash around with the others.

"Now that is not something you see every day," Lachlan said with a chuckle.

"How about it, Mags? Should we join them?" Atlas asked.

"No thanks. If it's okay with Lachlan, I'd like to shift and go down to the beach."

Lachlan scowled, then softened as he seemed to consider her request. "I suppose that depends on what you are."

"A horse," she said matter-of-factly.

"Oh, in that case, sure. But best to take someone with you. I don't want anyone walking by and thinking you're wild and try to tame you." He shuddered at the thought.

"As if they could catch me," Mags said with a mischievous grin.

"How about the rest of you? Atlas?"

"Bear."

"Mirage?"

"Wolf," I admitted without going into details.

"I didn't want to assume."

I just shrugged. What did it matter when I couldn't even shift.

"Can we go to the beach now?" Mags asked.

"Of course," Lachlan said, but he made no move to join us.

"By ourselves?" she clarified.

"Yes. You don't need my permission. I'm only concerned about safety matters, like shifting in front of humans or something. And watch out for each other. They said the water was pretty calm on this part of the island, but you never know. And if you can't swim, please don't go out too deep."

"Yes, sir," she said, and then grabbed my hand and dragged me along before he could change his mind. Atlas followed us.

Before we left the property, and under the cover of some low bushes, Mags shifted. She was a magnificent black horse.

"Beautiful," I whispered.

She whinnied and nodded her big head before trotting ahead of us, leading the way.

When we reached the sand, I froze and nearly jumped back. I took off the shirt I was wearing, feeling a little awkward and exposed in the small bikini that was barely covering any part of me. Atlas didn't even look my way which made me feel a little better, at least. I wasn't used to seeing him shirtless in just shorts either. Upon my first arrival to the collection I'd thought him to be the most handsome man in the world, but he paled in comparison to Colin.

"It sort of squishes between your toes," Atlas said sounding amused. "Relax. I've never felt it before either."

It distracted me from my thoughts. To hide my blush, I leaned over and scooped up a handful to examine it closely, mesmerized by all the tiny particles.

"It's hot," I whined a few feet in.

"Maybe it'll be cooler by the water. Let's go."

He grabbed my hand, and we ran towards the water while Mags took off down the beach, but not too far before turning back.

Atlas was right. When we reached the wet sand, it was much cooler and soothing, but also very different than the dry sand. It was more mud-like, but not really. I had no idea how to describe it.

We just stood there letting the water ebb and flow until our feet started to sink in the sand.

"This is amazing," he finally said.

"It really is. Did you ever imagine such a thing?"

"Never." He looked around and then leaned over to whisper. "No one's watching us. We should make a run for it while we can."

"And just leave the others behind?"

"They'll be fine. This could be our chance at real freedom."

"The trackers, Atlas. Be serious. He can still come for us."

"We'll cut them out of each other. It'll be fine."

It wasn't just that. I didn't think I could leave.

*Mate!* my wolf protested in my head as pictures of Colin flashed through my mind.

"You don't understand. It's not just them," I whispered. I didn't even understand what was happening between me and Colin. How the hell was I supposed to explain it to Atlas?

"He'll protect you, you know. I don't know if I trust all of them, but I doubt there's anything Colin wouldn't do for you."

My cheeks flushed with embarrassment.

"Hey, don't worry about it. He's your true mate, right?"

I shrugged. "I don't even really know what that means, but I have this like weird connection to him. I can't explain it, but I also can't walk away from it."

# Colin

## Chapter 15

I didn't like having Mirage out of my sight. It made me anxious. It was one thing when I could see her by the pool, but it was entirely different when she left with Atlas and Magnolia.

"What's up, T?" Grant asked.

"Bad news. We can't stay here."

"What? Why not?" I asked.

"Tarron is tracking the transportation team that their Collector hired. He's convinced this guy is personally coming after them. He was on route to California and then made an emergency stop just outside Vegas and has put in a reroute request. He's coming here. Tarron's trying to find ways to stall approvals and Patrick's calling in every favor we have, but if we stay here, there's a possibility he could be at our door by morning."

"The point of this is to hide San Marco. We need hops, and plenty of them. He'll know we aren't dropping them off because he's tracking them. But we need to keep him guessing to camouflage our mistake of taking them home without proper due diligence." Grant explained.

I sighed. "How long?"

"We'll give them an hour. Beckett and Grey are already working to get our flight plans set. They'll be off the books in case he has someone alerting him the way we do. Though I guess it doesn't matter much since he literally has a GPS right to our door," Taylor said in frustration.

"When can we get the trackers out?"

"We have a plan for that, but you're going to have to be patient."

Taylor nodded in agreement.

I felt like I was being partially kept in the dark and I didn't like it. Did they still not trust me? Things were different now. I had a reason to live and her name was Mirage. More importantly, there was nothing I wouldn't do to see her survive and thrive.

The kitchen was already stocked. I retrieved a case of cold Cokes and a large platter of fruits, cheeses, and crackers I'd found in the fridge and walked out to the pool deck.

"Drinks and snacks if anyone wants them," I called out, then stopped as I saw the comical menagerie swimming in the pool.

I wasn't even sure what some of the animals were, but they were a comical mix all swimming in the pool. Ned was the only one still in his skin.

"Is that Coke?" he asked, his eyes going wide as he licked his lips.

"Ice cold. Help yourself."

He stumbled over a chair trying to get to it as fast as he could. He quickly snatched one up, popped the lid, and tilted his head back for a long sip.

"Mmm, so good. I never thought I'd taste this again."

I couldn't even imagine Coke ever tasting quite that good. It made me sad for all of them, and angry that my mate had gone through all of this. I didn't know her full story yet, but one Collector was too many, and I vowed not to stop until every Collector was taken down for this.

Laughter caught my attention as I turned to see Magnolia, Atlas, and Mirage walking back from the beach. They looked so carefree here. I hated telling them we had to move on soon.

The way Mirage's oversized, wet T-shirt clung to her body distracted me as they approached. I cleared my throat. "There's snacks and cold drinks if you'd like," I said, pointing to the stuff I'd set out on the table.

"Mirage, you have to come into the pool. It's amazing," Gwen yelled.

When I turned to look back at the pool, the menagerie of animals had morphed back into humans as Ned passed around the sodas.

Mirage plucked a grape from the tray and popped it into her mouth as she sighed happily.

Damn. I couldn't take my eyes off of her, yet she didn't even seem to notice.

She licked her bottom lip, and I instantly grew hard. There was so much I wanted to know about my mate, but I also wanted her physically with a desperation that terrified me. The urge to claim her was stronger than I imagined it would be.

Atlas cannonballed into the pool and the splash of water did little to tame my desires. And then she slowly pulled off that damn shirt to reveal a bikini that barely concealed anything.

I growled.

"Shit. Guys, out," Atlas said.

"What the hell are you talking about?" Boris argued.

Atlas just smiled. "I'll tell you inside. Come on. Let the ladies have some time alone."

*Thank you,* I mouthed to him as he passed, earning me a solemn nod.

Lachlan on the other hand came and sat right in front me obscuring my view of my mate.

I growled, baring my teeth to him.

"Well I was going to ask if you were okay, but I can see you're not. Maybe we should talk about things."

I looked at him like he was crazy and then growled again when Mirage walked into the pool and out of my sight.

Taylor laughed, startling me from thoughts of ripping his throat out.

"Lachlan, sometimes you are so observant and other times you're a complete idiot. Come on inside and help us."

He genuinely looked confused.

"What did I do?" he whispered.

"The others left because he was feeling territorial with his mate in a swimsuit, and you stayed and blocked his sight of her."

"Oh. Well, shit. I screwed that one up, yeah?"

"Yeah."

She was still laughing when the door closed, and I tuned them out entirely letting my focus revert to my mate.

With long blonde hair and big blue eyes, she was beautiful. It brought peace to my wolf just looking at her, and that wasn't something I'd truly felt for far too long.

I had no idea how long I sat there staring at her, but a blush colored her cheeks whenever she looked at me. They were all whispering and laughing and every now and then I caught my name. I didn't care that they were talking about me.

Mirage looked up and caught my gaze. For a brief moment we seemed to be locked in this perfect bubble where only the two of us existed. It was a world I knew I could be happy in, like really happy. A place where the darkness wasn't threatening to consume me every second of my life. She was a spark of hope and light.

The others came back out and Grant popped my little Mirage bubble.

"Sorry to break up the party, but the plane's ready. We need you all to dry off and change so we can head back to the airfield," Grant told them.

"We aren't staying?" Gwen asked, sadly.

"Afraid not."

"But…" Ramona started to protest.

"No buts," I said. "We have to keep moving. Your Collector is en route and headed this way. We need to stay ahead of him."

"Can't we just remove these chips now?" Cypress asked.

I shook my head. "I'm sorry. We can't. Not yet. We have to protect all of you, but also need to clean up our mistake by hiding our home. We harbor a lot of witches there. We're concerned for their safety too."

"What if we made it appear like we were dropping off one of us at a time as we bounce around?" Atlas asked.

I certainly hadn't considered that or even knew what the plan was to get the trackers out of them. I turned to looked at Grant and Taylor for guidance. The others did too. This was much more in their realm of expertise than mine.

"Let me run it by Tarron," T said as she grabbed her phone and made the call immediately.

The girls got out and walked over to devour the food I'd set out. I had no doubt they were all worried about when the next time they'd eat would be, but there was no need. We'd take care of all that. I didn't tell them that though.

"We don't fully know what resources this guy has," Taylor said as she hung up the phone. "But Tarron believes it's worth a try. He's mapped out a crazy journey, but adding this level to it just might slow him up enough to pull this off. Who wants to be the first volunteer?"

"Me!" Mags shouted, practically knocking the others out of the way to get to her.

They all just chuckled.

"Sorry. I got a little taste of freedom going for a run on the beach in my coat and I will do anything for more of that."

"It should be Mirage," Atlas insisted.

Of course, I agreed with him. The sooner that device was out of her, the better as far as I was concerned.

"No, let Mags go first," my mate insisted.

"Okay," Grant said as he pulled out an antiseptic and wiped the bump concealing the chip. "This is going to sting."

"I don't care," she said.

Tears sprang to her eyes as he made a small incision and then pried the chip from her, but her smile only grew bigger. Two stitches later and it was done.

"That's it?" Ned asked.

"For the tracker, yes."

Taylor took a tracking detector and ran it over her body. "We got it."

"Is the tracker still active?" I asked.

She put her wand near it and it immediately lit up. "Yeah, it is."

"Good. Take it down the beach and leave it there."

"Active?" she asked.

"Definitely. I have a feeling this guy wants every single one of them back. It'll slow him down coming here and then searching for it."

"Bury it. And put a makeshift cross over it," Boris suggested. "He may or may not try to dig her body up. If he doesn't then he'll just assume she's dead. The next stop we'll break it in two and maybe he'll spend some time looking around the area trying to find one of us. We can hope."

"That could definitely buy us a bit more time. Good thinking," Grant agreed.

"Can I do it?" Mags surprised us by asking.

"You want to bury yourself?" Ned asked with a snort.

"Symbolically, yes. Burying the life I've lived and resurrected into a new and better one."

Mirage hugged her tightly. I couldn't imagine what they were going through.

A small group of them walked down the beach and buried the chip, setting it up like a makeshift grave. Mirage and I both stayed back.

"Are you okay?" I asked her.

She nodded. "I should change and get ready to leave."

I was hesitant to let her go, but I didn't stop her and I didn't follow her.

"How are you holding up?" Lachlan asked.

I groaned. "You're going to be asking me that every five seconds, aren't you?"

"Probably, yeah."

I sighed with frustration.

"So…? How are you doing?"

"You're impossible. I'm fine."

"Are you still having dark thoughts?"

"If you take into the fact that I want to rip out the throat of this guy chasing us, then yes."

"Interesting. A definite focus realignment."

Taylor laughed. "Trust me when I say finding his true mate is affecting that, Lachie. Someday, you'll understand."

# Mirage

## Chapter 16

I had never been so tired in my entire life. We'd left the beautiful island quickly after burying Magnolia's tracker. It hurt leaving that place where I'd felt safe and happy for the briefest moment.

Life had been a whirlwind since Colin stepped into it, but even more so after that. We'd gotten on a plane and flown for what felt like days stopping somewhere in Africa long enough to get out and stretch while they fueled up.

There we had removed Magnolia's tracker, carried it a few yards away, broke it and then left what looked like a crime scene of some sort of animal blood that had been waiting for us at the hanger.

Who were these guys? More importantly, who was Colin? If I stopped to think about him, it terrified me. I knew nothing about him, yet I was trusting him with my life as well as the lives of those I cared most about.

For the most part he was pretty quiet and kept to himself. He always had our backs and stood up to the others for us when needed. Not that it had been anything major, just little stuff like demanding we be allowed off of the plane for a few minutes at each stop.

After that first one, we made two more.

At the next, Cypress had her tracker removed. They'd gotten into a golf cart and drove it at a running pace before stopping and transferring to a car and driving away. Apparently, they'd broken her chip out in the middle of nowhere and left it there.

They'd explained that all of this was just to throw him off our trail or delay him looking for each of us.

He may be naïve, but he wasn't stupid. If he dug up the tracker for Gwen and found no body, then he'd be onto us and know we were removing the trackers. He wouldn't waste time on the others, he'd come after the majority. I was certain of it, but I didn't say anything. The others were too hopeful that it would work, and I didn't want to take that hope away from them.

On the last stop I was told we were still in Africa somewhere on the east coast. I didn't know where, and at this point places were meaningless to me. I didn't even bother paying attention. All I heard was that we were stopping for the night at a house.

Once again it was a big and fancy house, standing out amongst the tiny rundown buildings we drove by to get there. It was dark outside—really dark—but I could still make out just enough to know it was much of the same. I would have been fine with one of those tiny huts I saw, but Colin explained we needed a place large enough for all of us and that limited our options.

I didn't think he understood how many people could cram into a small space. Under normal circumstances for transport that I had experienced, all eight of us would have been shoved into a space about the size of the back bathroom in the bedroom of the plane. I couldn't fathom how big that was.

I'd really thought that the room my last Collector had given me was spacious, but I realized now that I had no idea what that word even meant.

Feeling exhausted, I wandered into the house and looked around. Lachlan was giving orders for sleeping arrangements and encouraging everyone to try to get some good sleep. We'd be heading right back out in the morning, but they all thought we needed a good night of rest first.

The excitement of everything was starting to wane. I found myself more nervous and unsure of everything as the days went on.

"Um, you didn't say where I'm supposed to sleep."

"We put your things in Colin's room," Grant said like that was the most natural thing in the world as he pointed me into that direction.

Fear and confusion must have shown on my face because Lachlan immediately jumped to my defense.

"Unless that makes you uncomfortable, then we can move you in with the girls, or have Grant and Colin share a room and you can stay with Taylor."

"Like hell she can," Grant protested earning him an elbow to the gut. "What?"

"We're on a mission."

"Sweet T, don't do this to me."

"Don't you Sweet T me. You know the mission rules."

"B-but this is different."

She snorted. "No, it's not. Would you rather stay with me, Mirage?"

Grant was shaking his head no behind her back and I felt bad for even thinking of saying yes. In truth I wasn't exactly comfortable with her. Her role in the witch auction was still a bit unsettling to me no matter how many times they tried to explain they were buying witches to set them free. Nothing in life was free. I knew that better than most.

"I'm fine with Colin," I finally said.

It was a little unnerving just how true those words were. For some reason just being near him brought me comfort in a way I didn't understand.

"Well, if you change your mind, or need to talk, I'll be on the couch tonight," Lachlan said.

Colin stepped out of the bedroom while we were talking and started to laugh. "Doing a little reverse role play tonight or something, Lachie?"

Grant and Taylor laughed right along with him.

I didn't get what was so funny, and I guessed Lachlan didn't find it all that funny either because he turned and flipped him the bird.

I gasped, waiting for a fight to break out, but Colin and the others just laughed harder as he kept walking away.

"We're going to say goodnight now. But Mirage, if you're uncomfortable at any time, we're just right across the hall. I don't mind sharing and kicking this guy out," Taylor told me with a warm smile.

I really wanted to like her. I just wished we'd met under different circumstances. Maybe then it wouldn't be quite so unsettling.

"We're in here," Colin said.

His voice sent a warm feeling through my body.

"Okay," I managed to say.

I'd slept in his bed that first night and nothing had happened. For some reason I trusted him more than I'd ever trusted anyone in my entire life, and it was scaring the shit out of me. I didn't even know him. Not really. It made no sense.

I'd learned a few things talking on the plane, like how he was an only child and had lost his parents at a young age. He had been raised by his grandparents and it was their house that he lived in, having inherited it when they passed.

He was a personal trainer and worked at Westin Force on Delta team. I learned they didn't often travel like this, but an exception was made for him because of me.

Everyone knew we were mates, and I barely even understood what that meant. I kept meaning to ask Mags what she knew, but there hadn't been a chance. All shifters had some level of accelerated hearing and there was no way I was going to ask with everyone listening in, especially when Colin was there.

I blushed at the thought.

"Your stuff is on the chair and the bathroom is just through that door."

"Um, okay," I said before retrieving something to sleep in and the toothbrush and toothpaste I'd picked up when we stopped back on the island. "I'll just be a few minutes."

"Take your time."

I didn't want to push my luck, but inside the bathroom was the biggest tub I'd ever seen, and it was calling to me but so was sleep. I'd only ever seen something like it on TV. What would it be like to soak in there with candles lit all around and maybe a book to read or soft music in the background?

Shaking my head, I laughed at myself. I'd clearly seen one movie too many. Now was not the time to be pampered, though this adventure we were on sure made me feel like I was being pampered. I never dreamed I would see such wonders and walk so freely.

Instead of indulging and risking getting in trouble, I dared to take a quick shower before changing into the silky clothes and getting ready for bed.

I was nervous walking out, knowing Colin would be sharing a bed with me. It wasn't a normal kind of nervousness though. There was a thrill of excitement coursing through me, and I didn't understand why.

*Mate,* my wolf kept reminding me.

Colin wasn't in bed when I stepped back into the bedroom. Nope, he was standing there in just a pair of shorts, no shirt. I'd seen the other guys like that at the beach and in the pool, I'd even seen others fully naked before shifting, but my cheeks didn't heat and my pulse didn't rise seeing them like that.

I couldn't stop staring at him, and in two strides he closed the gap between us and wrapped me up in his arms. I gulped hard as his lips crashed against mine.

I sighed and started to kiss him back before my brain engaged with what was actually happening. Maybe I didn't know what I was doing, but my lips did. I craved him with a desperation I didn't know was possible.

When a soft moan escaped me and his tongue swept into my mouth, I froze. Reality came crashing in on me and I started to panic.

My body went rigid, and I pushed him away from me as hard as I could looking around the room for a safe place to hide.

Engaging my powers to conceal myself I ran to the corner and shrank to the floor as my knees came up to my chest, covering my ears, and closing my eyes as I rocked back and forth.

"Mirage, what's wrong?" Colin asked. He sounded worried and a little confused.

I dared to open my eyes and yelped when I saw him kneeling in front of me.

"You can see me?"

"No, but my wolf can sense you. Why are you hiding from me?"

"You kissed me," I shouted.

He looked even more confused. "I did. I just wasn't quite expecting this sort of reaction. Talk to me."

I shook my head even though he couldn't see it.

"Mirage, please. Talk to me."

I recalled my powers and faced him, still balled up in the corner and shaking all over.

He looked horrified and jumped back as fur started sprouting up his arms.

I gasped.

My fear must have subdued him some as he gulped in deep breaths and slowly regained control of himself.

"I'm sorry. I didn't mean to scare you. I just don't understand what happened."

"You kissed me."

He gave a sheepish grin. "I remember that part."

I glared at him in shock. "I know what comes next. I'm not a complete idiot."

"What exactly do you think comes next?"

Memories that haunted my darkest nightmares surfaced as I tried not to freak out.

"Mirage?" he asked softly.

"Sex. That's what comes next. Sex, and blood, and screams."

I shook all over feeling like the helpless little girl I'd once been and hating myself for it. I was stronger than this.

Through clenched teeth he growled. His fists were balled up at his sides.

"Who hurt you?"

My eyes widened as I realized how angry he sounded.

"No one," I admitted. "And no one ever will."

He started to relax a little.

"No one?"

I shook my head. "When they tried to come for me, I would cloak myself so they couldn't find me. It got me in trouble sometimes and kicked out of at least one collection, but I made a promise that no one would ever hurt me like that. I'm never having sex."

# Colin

## Chapter 17

*Never having sex.* Those words echoed through my head. Holy shit. What was I going to do? I wanted her so bad it hurt. No, I didn't just want her, I desperately needed her. *Never?*

"Not all sex is bad or painful like that. Only monsters would take someone against their will. Sex should be sacred and good."

She shook her head, and, at that moment, she looked so young and scared. I just wanted to pull her into my arms and hold her forever. Or kiss away all that darkness and show her how very different sex could be. I didn't dare make a move towards her again though.

"You really need to talk to someone about this, Mirage. This isn't healthy. I don't know what you saw or experienced in there, but it's clear it was bad. I wish to God I could have been there to save you sooner. Maybe you should talk to Lachlan. He's really helped me out, though if you tell him I said that I'll deny it."

"Lachlan? Why would I want to talk to him?"

"He's sort of like the Force's shrink."

"Shrink?"

"Yeah, a psychologist. He's helped a lot of people who have experienced trauma. He helps you talk things through and get to the root of the problem. It's not like he can fix it, but he can help you fix it, if that makes sense. And he's a good listener if you're willing to talk, and an arrogant pain in the ass who will patiently sit there and wait if you're not."

She nibbled on her lower lip, and I wanted to reach out and caress it, but her response to me kissing her had traumatized me a bit too.

What the hell had they done to her in there? I needed to know if we were ever to move past this.

"It's late. Why don't you take the bed? I'll sleep on the floor tonight."

"What?" she asked, looking torn and confused.

"Mirage, I will never purposefully hurt you in any way. You are the most precious person in the world to me. Do you even understand what it means to be true mates?"

She sucked in a sharp breath and nodded, but the look on her face wasn't convincing.

"I know enough."

"Do you want to talk about it?"

She shook her head. "Not tonight. I'm really tired, Colin."

I gave her a sad smile and nodded resolutely. Cautiously, I held out my hand to her and helped her to her feet and then into bed. I tucked her in but didn't dare join her. Instead, I stretched out on the chair and footstool next to the bed.

"Sweetheart, how long have you been in the collection?" I asked softly.

"Only a few months for this one. I liked it there though. The others took me in like family. And he never really asked for much. It wasn't so bad."

My heart broke for her. To think that was enough for her. I supposed the bar for me had been set pretty low, but it hurt knowing she'd had to live like that at all. Still, I needed to know more.

"And before that?"

She sighed. "I was first taken at age eight. I've been bounced around to lots of different collections. Some aren't so bad, others were... hard..." she whispered letting her voice trail off.

I gritted my teeth and took a deep breath. Freaking out and losing it wasn't going to help us any.

"Do you even know how old you are?"

"Twenty-eight," she said. "This year marked my twentieth year of collections."

"How can you be sure?"

She took a deep breath and let it go. "I just know."

There was something she wasn't saying, but I didn't feel like now was the time to press her on it.

"I'm about to turn thirty. I've been kind of dreading it until now."

"Until now? What changed?"

I looked over and saw her watching me curiously.

"You," I whispered.

We were silent for a long time as we just watched each other. It wasn't awkward or uncomfortable in any way. I could look at her for days and never tire of it. She didn't seem in a hurry to look away from me either. Despite the little kissing mishap of earlier, it gave me a bit of hope that just maybe we could work through things.

She cleared her throat. "That chair doesn't look very comfortable. You should come to bed."

"Sweetheart, I don't want to make you uncomfortable in any way. As long as you're near and I can occasionally touch you, I'll be okay."

My touch had never seemed to bother her, until that kiss. She told me no one had touched her, which only meant that she must have witnessed things I couldn't even fathom. I knew I could show her that there was a better way, that sex didn't have to be this terrifying and ugly thing she'd made it out to be, but I was scared of the rejection again if I tried. So I wasn't going to push her. I could be patient and let her come to me.

Baby steps.

"I feel safer when you touch me," she blurted out. "It doesn't make sense. I don't like people in my personal space… except you."

I almost didn't make out those last two words because she said them so softly.

In the blink of an eye I was on the other side of the bed sliding under the sheets next to her.

It was a start.

"Can I hold you?" I asked her.

She didn't hesitate to nod and even launched herself into my arms as she snuggled down using my chest as her pillow.

My wolf settled and I instantly calmed down.

It might take time, but I had to believe we were going to be okay.

She took a deep breath like she was sniffing me.

"I like the way you smell. It comforts me too," she admitted.

"It's all part of the mating bond," I told her honestly.

"When I was little and new to my first collection, there was an older woman there named Delilah. She would tell me fairy tales each night and I remember one about true mates. It was about a girl who bravely went out into the world and searched high and low for her one true mate."

"Did she find him?"

"Yes, but an ogre cut off his head and she was confined to a cell to live out her days brokenhearted."

I chuckled. "That's a terrible story."

She shrugged, but I could feel her smile against my chest.

"She said it was because you only get one true mate, no matter what, you're stuck with him for better or worse until death do you part."

"What else do you know about true mates?"

"Everyone says you're mine."

I looked down to find her big blue eyes staring back at me with so many questions swirling within them. I was mesmerized.

"I am."

"How can you be sure?"

"For one, my wolf tells me on a regular basis. He doesn't like that I haven't claimed you already."

She started to stiffen and pull away, but I held her tight.

"That's not a bad thing, Mirage. Think of it like this, right now there's this invisible string tying us together and pulling us closer. It's the start of a bond. Someday, when you're ready, I'll claim you by biting your neck and marking you forever. You'll do the same to me and then we'll be bonded for life."

"I've never heard it put that way before. Why me?"

"Because you're mine, and I'm meant to be yours."

"Mine?" she asked softly. "I've never had anything that belongs to me."

"I belong to you," I told her softly.

She stared up into my eyes and then nodded. She reached her hand up and caressed my cheek as a sly smile crossed her face. "All mine," she whispered.

When she laid back down, I dared a quick kiss to the top of her head. She had never really seemed to freak out about those kisses at least.

As we drifted off to sleep, I could hear our hearts beating in unison.

"Mine," I whispered before allowing sleep to consume me.

*****

My dick jerked and then it was pushed down as I heard a soft giggle. I went from fast asleep to wide awake in split second.

A mess of blonde hair splayed out across my chest and a small hand reached out and touched me once more. It was then I realized that my boxers were pushed down, and I was fully exposed and hard enough to pound nails.

I was so shocked that I thought I must still be dreaming.

But then she wrapped her hands around my shaft and squeezed.

I moaned and she jumped slightly.

"Oh, you're awake. Sorry. At first, I thought you might have a rat or something in your pants because it kept moving like there was something in there, but when I checked it was just your penis. I've never seen one so hard before. Is this normal?"

I gulped hard as she squeezed me.

"Um, yup. That's normal. Especially first thing in the morning sleeping with a beautiful woman wrapped around me all night," I muttered.

"Do you know why men and woman are made differently?"

It was such an innocent question, and I never wanted her to feel silly or naïve for asking me something. Hell, she'd been eight years old when she was captured and clearly, she had a warped sense of sex. Who really knew what they had told her?

But it was hard to think as she continued to stroke me seemingly fascinated by the way it reacted.

"Um, yeah, men and women are designed differently to fit together as one."

"Like a puzzle?"

"Um, yup, like a puzzle."

I needed to tell her to stop before things went too far. I was only flesh and bones. I couldn't handle but so much without nature taking course.

"So where does this fit into me exactly?" she asked.

I wanted to chuckle at her sweetness. Was I even the right person to try and explain the birds and the bees to her? But if not me, then who?

She gripped me hard at my base and then slowly pulled her hand upwards until I popped free. She grinned up at me when it jumped out of my control.

"So?" she asked, giving me her full attention now.

"Where, yeah, well, um, you're sort of built different in this area."

"I don't have a penis," she agreed.

"No, but you do have a special place there."

Before I could stop her, she pulled off her pants and fully exposed herself to me.

"Show me," she insisted.

"Are you sure about this?"

She had said she never wanted to have sex before, but I was beginning to realize she had no idea what that even meant. Sexual exploration and curiosity were normal. I just need to be honest with her and it would be fine.

"I'm sure. Please."

I tried to point it out to her.

"Where?" she asked.

Without thinking I touched her.

"Right here," I said in a deep voice.

She was so wet and ready for me.

A soft gasp escaped her. "That feels good," she said, pulling my hand back to her when I tried to retreat. "Why does that feel so good?"

"Because we were made for each other. It should always feel good."

She grinded herself against my hand until I slipped one finger inside of her.

"Oh," she said as her eyes widened. "Like two pieces of a puzzle," she whispered to herself.

Before I could stop her, she grabbed my dick and slowly lowered herself onto me. I felt the final barrier for the briefest moment as she buried me fully within her and then looked up triumphantly.

"I got it."

I didn't know what to do or say. I knew what I wanted to do but had no idea what I should do in this situation. It felt a lot like I could be taking advantage of her, even though she was technically the one taking advantage of me.

"Now what?" she asked, and I wasn't sure if she was talking to me or herself.

Either way, she was figuring it out on her own as I laid there frozen and she started to move.

"Mmm, this feels nice," she said. "Is this part of the bond thing you were talking about?"

"Uh, it can be, but not necessarily."

"Oh."

In her frustration to figure things out she really started to find a rhythm that called me to act.

"Mirage, are you sure this is what you want?"

"Yes," she said.

My hands bit into her hips as I started to move with her. She was so tight and felt so good, squeezing me with each thrust that I wasn't sure how long I could handle it. Still, even though she was clearly not aware of us having sex, she was all in. This was her first time, and it was up to me to make her feel good about it.

She was so beautiful and completely uninhibited as she sought her first orgasm.

"So good," she moaned.

"You just do whatever makes you feel good, sweetheart. I'm right here with you, but you're in full control."

Something flashed in her eyes. Empowerment. I doubt either of us knew she needed to hear those words, but it was obvious she did.

"Does this feel good to you too?" she asked me.

"Everything you do to me feels good. Every time you touch me it feels good."

"Will you touch me?" she asked almost shyly.

She may not have known what she needed exactly, but as her breathing quickened and her motions became more erratic, I knew she was close to her first orgasm.

"I've got you," I said, pressing my thumb to her apex and drawing circles with it.

She jerked and moaned loudly as she rode me hard, pulling me along with her.

Her whole body tensed, and I thrust up into her as she fell apart and collapsed onto my chest breathing hard.

I pumped into her twice more and then let go.

She moaned again and her eyes widened with questions as she looked up at me, but they were also wild and free.

"That was amazing. I never knew something like that existed. You really are made just for me."

I grinned and brushed her hair out of her face. I wanted to kiss her so badly, but first I had to explain what had just happened.

"Baby, we need to talk."

Her face frowned. "Did I do something wrong?"

"No, not at all."

She started to withdrawal from me.

"Hey, don't. I'm yours, remember? You can touch me and ride me anytime you need."

"Then what's wrong?"

I sighed. "Last night when I kissed you…"

She jerked away and her cheeks burned.

"Don't pull away from me, please. This is important. You said you never wanted to have sex before."

"And I meant it. I'm never letting someone hurt me like that."

"Did you ever see someone having sex?" I asked cautiously.

"Well, no, but I heard plenty."

So, I was right. She really didn't have any idea what she was doing.

"Mirage, remember when I said some sex is good and some can be bad?"

She nodded.

"The sex you heard was clearly bad. That was someone being forced to do something they didn't want to do. Do you understand that?"

She nodded again.

"What we just did, baby, that was the good kind of sex."

Her eyes nearly bugged out her head. "Th-that was sex?"

I nodded. "I'm so sorry. You needed to explore that side of you, and I'll always be here whenever you need me in that way, but that was sex. When it's with the right person, it should feel good, great even. It should never hurt you. Do you understand?"

She pulled her knees up to her chest and started to rock. It broke my heart to see her that way, but it was clear she was considering everything I'd just told her and processing the emotions of it all.

"So that was it? That was sex?"

"That was sex."

"Huh." She relaxed and stretched back out beside me in bed. "Well, I guess if that was sex, then I want more of it, as long as it's just with you."

I growled and grinned, fighting the urge to kiss her. "Only ever with me, because you're mine."

A part of me feared that my possessiveness over her would scare her. She wasn't mine to own and put in a room or on display, she was mine to love and protect, to cherish always. Could she feel the difference?

"And you're mine," she whispered, hugging me tightly.

I checked the clock and saw we still had an hour or so before we needed to start packing.

She reached down and started to play with me once more as I groaned.

"It's not hard anymore."

I laughed. "You sort of took care of that already."

"Well, when will it come back again?"

"You keep touching me like that and it'll be sooner than you think."

She gave me an evil smirk.

I groaned. "You're going to be the death of me woman."

Mirage stopped and whipped her head towards me with a horrified look on her face.

I reached out and caressed her cheek. "That was meant to be a joke. I'm not actually dying anytime soon."

Pausing, I let that sink in for a minute. I was never suicidal, but I was accepting of possible death. That wasn't okay with me now.

"It wasn't a funny joke," she said.

"I know. I'm sorry. You're just driving me crazy in a really good way. When you touch me, it feels so good. I want so badly to touch you and show you how good you can feel too, but I'm scared you'll freak out."

She considered that for a moment. "I don't know if I will or not. I wasn't scared at all when we had sex. It felt great."

I grinned. "Good. That's how it should always be. I don't ever want to hurt you."

"I believe you."

I smiled. "Can I…"

The alarm on my phone sounded, cutting off my question. I groaned in frustration.

"What?" she asked.

"Later. That's our signal to get moving."

We had just finished dressing, still smiling at each other the whole time. Every time she looked at me a cute blush crossed her face. She looked genuinely happy, and that made me happier than I ever imagined. But then Taylor barged in.

"Good you're ready. We have a situation."

My wolf spiked for control at the tone of her voice, I pushed him back and took a few deep breaths clenching and unclenching my fists at my sides.

"What is it?"

"He's here, hot on our trail. His plane landed ten minutes ago."

"Why am I just hearing about this?"

She looked back and forth between me and Mirage and then cleared her throat. "Because you were, um, indisposed at the time. We were rather hoping you would have sealed your bond, but I can sense you haven't."

I closed my eyes trying not to be embarrassed at finding out everyone in the house had been listening in. I growled at her.

"Relax. We're happy for you both. Grant and I just had the misfortune of being next door. And now isn't the time to worry about it. Grab your things and get to the van. The others are waiting."

Mirage took our things as I did a quick sweep of the room. I didn't have time to wipe it clean or dispose of the evidence of our lovemaking.

"It's okay. Cleaners are already here. I'll tell them to start in here."

"Thanks."

"Now move."

# Mirage

## Chapter 18

The others were already waiting for us. My friends looked terrified but curious as I clung to Colin.

"What's happening? Is he really here?"

He looked down at me and nodded. "T wouldn't lie about something like that."

"The important thing is for everyone to remain calm and do exactly as we say. We weren't expecting company today, but it's okay. We can work with this. It's a tight window, but we've got this," Lachlan optimistically told us.

No one else talked on the drive, though I tried not to freak out when we pulled up to a large freight ship. I'd once been transported in a steel box on one for two months during a relocation. There had been twenty of us there and a bit of straw, like cattle. We'd had to designate one corner for the bathroom and the stench was unbearable. It still made me gag just thinking about it.

I shook my head and froze, begging Colin not to make me go through it again.

"I can't. Please don't make me."

He wrapped his arms around me, but I only mildly calmed from his touch this time. I was on the verge of passing out.

"Please," I begged.

"Grant?" he asked, his voice filled with concern. It dawned on me that he was worried about me. He actually cared about me.

"This is the best chance we have. I'm sorry. We have to get on the boat."

The others complied and followed. They hadn't been through what I'd been through. They didn't understand what came next.

I got woozy and ran to the edge to puke in the water. Colin stayed right there rubbing my back and holding my hair back.

"Sweetheart, it's okay. I'll be right here with you every step of the way."

Tears burned my eyes as I resolved myself to fate once more. They escaped, streaming down my cheeks as he gently swiped them away with the pad of his thumb.

"Hold my hand and don't let go. I'm here and I'm not going anywhere. We do this together, okay?"

"It's not okay, but I don't have a choice."

"There's always a choice."

The others were already on the boat when Taylor came running out.

"He's not going to the house. He's coming straight here. We have to move quickly. It's time."

Colin nodded and swooped me up into his arms.

"Just close your eyes. It'll all be over soon."

I didn't know what that meant, but I relinquished full control to him as I buried my face in his chest and cried while he walked us onto the boat, down a long hall, and deep into the bowels of the beast.

Grant and the others were there next to a group of pigs.

"Thank you," Atlas said, shaking his hand.

"Follow Grey out with the others. Move quickly." Then he looked up at us. "Finally. My last patient. Set her down."

Colin did as Grant instructed, but true to his word, he never left my side. He quickly removed the tracking chip from my arm and then implanted it into one of the pigs. Before stitching me up.

"That's it. Let's go."

Colin tried to carry me again, but I shook him off and just held his hand for dear life instead.

"Two of his men just boarded. He's still on shore," I heard Taylor's soft voice via Colin's earpiece. "Get down now and move quickly to your left."

He put his finger to his mouth and covered me as we did what we were told.

"Drop."

We did.

"They're on your nine, hold for my mark."

Grant winked at me and grinned.

"Go."

As if they were fully synchronized, Grant and Colin moved as one with me wedged between them. It was then I saw the pistol in Grant's hand as he passed his bag to Colin.

Without saying a word, I understood that Colin was telling me to breathe in and out slowly. I knew I was on the verge of hyperventilating.

"There's a container twenty feet to your right. Get there. Now. Go. Go. Go," she instructed.

I froze at the door shaking my head violently. I couldn't go in there. I couldn't do it again. My stomach started to retch again.

Colin got Grant's attention and called it off.

"You have no choice. Now," T yelled.

I was just about to protest when Colin kissed me, wrapping his arms around me and pulling me into the container with him as Grant followed, chuckling, and closed the door behind us.

I was lost in that kiss. His lips were more demanding this time, but I was already too freaked out to panic any further. Instead,

I closed my eyes and kissed him back like this was my last moment of life, because it very well could be.

"Did the others get out?" Grant whispered.

"All of them," she assured us. "And you will too."

"Where the hell are they?" I heard an all too familiar voice yell. "They have to be here. Keep searching. I don't know how they're screwing up the location, but they're here. I can feel it. Come out my pets. Come out wherever you are."

Suddenly my whole body was gripped in pain as spasms racked my body from the base of my neck down my spine.

He was close enough for me to hear even through the steel cage we were in. I couldn't cry out and lead him right to us. I had to protect myself—and my mate.

My hands fisted in Colin's shirt as he held me. Fresh tears slid down my cheeks. But I gritted my teeth and refused to cry out from the pain.

"Grant," he whispered in a voice too low for humans to hear. "Help."

"What the hell?" he whispered back.

"It's that implant we told you about. He's close enough to activate it."

"We have to get her out of here, T. Find us an exit," Grant barked.

"I'm on it. Going to rattle the beehive a bit."

"Let me clarify, T. We want out of here alive."

"Like I'd ever let anything happen to you."

"I love you, too."

In the distance a loud voice shouted. "Who the hell are you and what are you doing on my ship?"

"I'll handle this," the Collector said from what sounded like just outside our door, but he thankfully seemed to stop holding down the button of pain.

I gasped for breath trying not to make a sound. I felt weak and exhausted. Getting hit down my spinal column always did that to me.

Colin's arms tightened around me giving me strength.

"You are hiding something of mine, and I will not leave until I find it."

The arrogance in his voice made me cringe.

A gun fired multiple rounds, and I heard the Collector scream.

"Calm down. I have money, lots of money. I'll pay whatever you want."

"This ship is pulling out in five minutes. If you stay, you live with the pigs. Money don't mean shit at sea. Get them off my boat."

There was a skirmish, more gunfire, but this time it seemed to come from all around.

Taylor laughed. "Prepare to move."

"Can you walk?" Colin whispered.

"As long as he doesn't click that button again."

"No," Grant said. "Don't even think about it. This is an extraction only at this point. Are we clear?"

Colin growled. I had no idea what transpired between them.

"I'm serious," Grant warned, and he sounded like he meant it too.

"You're clear, come out and to your left along the wall as quickly as possible. The captain's men are keeping them busy. Drop down into the holding tank. We'll wait out our time there."

"On your mark," Grant said.

"Go already. Now."

With a chuckle he quietly slid the door open and let Colin and I pass first before closing it behind us. I could breathe a bit easier once out of that metal box. They once again kept me between them as they moved together following Taylor's instructions without question or pause. Colin dropped down in the holding tank first, and then Grant gave me a little shove forcing me to follow. Then he joined us, closing and locking it above.

Once again we were trapped.

"Are you okay?" Atlas whispered as he pulled me from Colin's arms earning himself a menacing growl.

"I'm okay. Did you all get shocked?"

"No. What?"

"He's here and he's looking for us. They have guns."

"Don't panic," Lachlan said. "It's all going to be okay. He can't track you here any longer. The captain knows we're here and he will protect us. We have a short day's ride, and then tonight under a cloud of darkness we'll move on, and you'll be safe and free to live your lives without fear of him finding you."

We all looked skeptical, but no one said a word.

"What if he doesn't get off this ship?" I whispered.

"Then that asshole is in for a long six-week journey to China," Beckett said with a laugh.

I froze. "But you said we're getting off tonight."

"We are. Just relax and trust us. We're holding watch, but no one is getting to you without a blood bath," Colin said darkly.

I shivered at the cold tone in his voice, and I absolutely believed every word of it.

"I know this isn't the most comfortable place to be but try to settle in and relax. There's a few bunks and some cots to rest on. We'll wake you when it's time to go."

"And a bathroom?" I asked, my voice shaky even to my own ears.

"It's right here," Taylor assured me, opening a door to prove it.

My whole body sank in relief and tears sprang to my eyes once more.

"Thank you," I told her, surprising us all by leaving Colin's side to hug her. She couldn't possibly know how much it meant to me.

The rest of the day passed by uneventfully. Grey had gone back up to talk to the captain and some of his men. The Collector and two of his men had stayed and begun searching every inch of the ship, demanding containers be opened, until at last the men grew tired of his games and shoved him into a mostly empty one and locked the three of them inside.

It was probably wrong of me to feel badly for him. I'd lived that nightmare and wouldn't wish it on my worst enemy, not even him.

When I told the others that, Grey assured me that it was only temporary.

"They're just keeping them occupied. They'll let them out tomorrow after we're long gone."

"But we've already set sail. We're in the middle of the ocean by now. How are we going to get off this boat?" Ramona demanded.

"It's all taken care of. You just have to have a little faith right now."

Colin found a deck of cards to pass the time. Most of the others had long since fallen asleep, but I couldn't even if I tried. Not here. Not on this ship. It was taking everything in my power not to hyperventilate or throw up again.

It was funny. For a girl who'd spent most of her life in captivity without issue, I found it ironic that boats would be my undoing.

A little after midnight, Grey walked around waking everyone. And soon we were shuffled out a door and lowered onto an emergency raft. I could see lights twinkling in the distance so I knew we couldn't be that far from shore.

Was this the plan? Just leave the ship and return to shore?

I wasn't even given enough time to freak as I was loaded onto the small boat. Once we were all on, Beckett took us to shore. He parked on a beach. I couldn't really see anything nearby.

"We did it!" Grant yelled as everyone cheered, but I stood there completely mesmerized staring up into the sky.

"There are so many stars," I said quietly.

The rest of them settled down quickly to listen and then look up.

"Wow," Mags said. "I've never seen anything so beautiful."

"It looks like it goes on forever," Cypress added.

"I never thought I'd see the night sky like this again," Boris said.

Ned started to get choked up. "It's beautiful."

Ramona held her arms out and twirled around as she looked up. "I don't know what's going to happen next or where we end up, but right here, right now, I actually feel free."

"You are free now. All of you," Colin said.

"We can take you anywhere you'd like to go. With the trackers removed and our trail covered, there's no way he'll ever find you again," Beckett assured us.

"I want to go home," Boris said.

"We can make that happen," Lachlan assured him.

My heart sank. "We're not staying together?"

"I have a mate back home that I miss very much. I need to get home to her."

"You do? You never told us."

"It's not something I talk about, but yes."

"A true mate?" I asked him.

"A true mate. I think you know what that means."

I looked up at Colin. I still didn't fully understand it, but I was beginning to.

# Colin

## Chapter 19

We spent the rest of the night on that tiny island somewhere in the Pacific and then Beckett and Grey got us the hell out of there.

The flight back was quiet and uneventful. I didn't get any time alone with my mate and still had so much to discuss with her. This time we were headed home for good. It got me wondering, where did she come from? Did she even know what pack she belonged to? Did she have family still praying for her return? Would she even want to look for them?

It didn't feel right asking her in front of everyone. I had no idea how much she had or hadn't shared with her friends.

"Buckle up, we'll be landing shortly." Beckett's voice rang out through the intercom.

"What happens now?" Gwen asked.

"Well, we'll ask you all to stick around a few days. Our team leaders will want to talk with you, it's nothing to worry about, just a typical debriefing. They'll be asking about your past inside the collections and anything you know about them that may help us rescue others," Taylor explained.

"But we don't know anything," Cypress insisted.

"You probably know a lot more than you realize," she said with a smile.

"But it's all voluntary," Lachlan interrupted. "If you aren't comfortable talking about it, no one will force you to. What you share with us could help save others, though."

"Okay, but then what?" Gwen asked.

"That's up to you," I told her.

"To me?"

"Yes. Each of you can decide where you want to go and what you want to do next. We've explained that. Boris wants to go home. The rest of you will have to decide for yourself."

Boris started to sob. It sobered us all.

"You really mean it? I can go home?"

"Yes, you're going home. Archie handles security and logistics for Westin Force. He's already searching for your family and getting things lined up for your return. You'll all be issued cell phones and have temporary housing while you consider your options."

"What if we don't have anywhere to go?" Ned asked. "Then what?"

"You are welcome to stay in San Marco," Lachlan told him.

Atlas snorted. "Right. They'll just let us move into a wolf pack. That's insane. What about those of us that aren't wolves?"

"I'm not a wolf," he surprised them by saying.

"You're not? What are you?" Ramona asked.

"I'm a dingo."

She rolled her eyes.

"Same thing. You're close enough. I'm a bear. A wolf pack would never welcome a bear into its territory," Atlas insisted.

I chuckled.

"We already have one family of bears living there. Why not another?" I told him.

"What? You have bears living in wolf territory? Are you serious?"

"Westin Force is made up of the best of the best, regardless of species," Grant explained. "Baine is on my team, Bravo, which has a mix of all different kinds of shifters. Let's see, we have gorillas, a bear, a fox, and even a human."

"Hold up, a fox? There are other fox shifters there?" Ned asked excitedly.

"Yes. In fact, Nonna has a bad habit of adopting them all." He smiled affectionately as I shook my head.

Nonna was a crazy old gossiping wolf who was good friends with my grandmother before she passed. She never had any children of her own, but for some reason when Tarron, the Bravo team fox, moved to town, she adopted him, and then his mate, and then her whole family. It was insane, but you couldn't convince that woman they weren't her own little family. The last time I saw her, she cornered me to show off a million pictures of her new great-grandbaby and kept asking me when I was going to have a pup of my own.

At the time I'd laughed at her. I had no plans to take a mate let alone become a dad, but looking at Mirage next to me, maybe that wouldn't be such a bad idea. I had a mate; it was only a matter of time before we made it permanent. We already had a great house plenty big enough for a whole litter of pups. Would she want kids with me?

I shook my head to clear it. This was insane. Why was I thinking about kids at a time like this?

I'd tuned out the entire conversation going on around me and was starting to freak out over the idea of being a dad…as long as Mirage was their mom.

Feeling the plane jerk as we touched down, I looked around me. No one seemed to notice I had zoned out as they excitedly talked about what they wanted to do most.

"I'm going to find some ice cream and then I'm going to eat it!" Magnolia exclaimed.

"Ice cream? What's that?" Mirage asked.

They all quieted as they turned to her with their jaws dropped.

She rolled her eyes and laughed. "I know what ice cream is. I'm not a complete idiot."

"But do you really?" Ned challenged.

"Have you ever tasted it?" Cypress asked.

She shrugged. "Not that I can remember. But I've seen them eat it in movies."

I checked my watch, seeing it was still early in the day.

"Okay, we'll go to headquarters for your debriefing, and then I'm taking you straight to the Cold Shack. They have the best ice cream in town."

"You mean it?"

"Yes. You're not going another day without experiencing ice cream."

"Can I come?" Magnolia asked.

"Me too," the others started proclaiming.

"Why don't we get everyone settled and then we'll figure out the ice cream situation. I know for a fact there's a stash of it down at headquarters too, and the Lodge almost always has it available," Grant said.

I scowled. "That's not the same. It's her first time."

He glared at me, but before anymore could be said, we had landed and the door was opening. Everyone grabbed their things and exited the plane. There was no hesitation or need to prod them. I supposed everyone was happy to be back on solid ground.

Michael and Silas were both anxiously awaiting our arrival.

"I hear everything went relatively smoothly," Michael said as he greeted us.

I shook his hand, and he pulled me into a hug.

"You look good. Less stressed."

I grabbed Mirage's hand and pulled her next to me.

"I know you've met, sorta, but in all the chaos, things got insane. Michael, this is my mate, Mirage. Babe, this is Michael, my team lead."

"Welcome home, Mirage. I'm very happy to officially meet you."

"Home?" she asked.

I sighed. "We haven't really discussed all of that yet."

"Oh. Well, okay. Um, you probably should handle that."

I laughed. "It's under control."

"Just don't go breaking his heart," he warned her.

She shot me a concerned look, but I just made a face and shook my head. There was no way I was diving into all of that here and now.

"Load up, we're all heading back to headquarters for debriefing," Silas ordered.

Atlas and Ned followed Mirage and I to my vehicle and climbed in without a world.

I tried not to be frustrated. I just spent more than twenty-four hours stuck on a plane with them. Call me selfish, but I would have liked a few minutes alone with my mate.

"Have you guys decided what you're going to do yet?" she asked them as I drove us to the Lodge.

"I'm going to ask to stay," Ned announced.

"Really?"

I didn't miss the excitement in her voice at his news. Did that mean she was planning to stay too? Was she excited to have a friend here? I damn sure hoped so.

"I haven't really decided yet. I'm certainly intrigued by the idea that there are bears and other animals actually living in a wolf pack. That's insane."

I shrugged. "We don't even think about it anymore. What does it matter what kind of shifter you are?"

He snorted. "Seriously? I mean, what would you do if Mirage had been a cat? That would be absurd."

"Actually, my Alpha's youngest brother is true mates with a black panther."

His mouth fell open and then he smiled and shook his head.

"Nah, you're just messing with me."

"I'm not kidding. Stick around and you'll see. We welcome everyone here."

Ned snorted. "Sure you do. Right up until they discover we're all a bunch of witches."

Mirage laughed. "You aren't even a witch, Ned."

"I know, but I am by association now. I've seen the other side and I can't unsee that. The way people think of you as different, scary even, an animal to be caged and paraded. It's disgusting. I'll admit, I used to be terrified of witches, but now I've earned my place as one and I'm going to protect you all from that sort of insanity ever happening again."

I could only imagine what they had all been through and the sort of bond something like that created.

"Yeah, why aren't you more freaked out about having a witch for a mate?" Atlas asked me.

I shrugged. "Witches are cool."

He snorted. "Said no one ever. We're hunted down and often murdered by our own kind and collected for show and bragging rights by the humans."

I growled, but Mirage reached out and touched me, calming me instantly.

"It's okay," she said. "He's right. And I am a witch. That should scare you."

"You're going to learn quickly that it takes a hell of a lot more than that to scare me."

The only thing I was truly afraid of was causing the death of someone I cared about, and now, losing my mate.

"No one will hurt you again," I softly told her. "Not ever."

"But you can't guarantee that," Atlas said. "Your Westin Force team already knows what we are. They'll either try to use us for our powers or kill us claiming they're scared of us."

"No one is killing anyone. On top of taking in refugees, many of whom we've rescued like you guys, Westin Pack has become a haven for witches. Has no one mentioned that to you guys?"

Ned growled. "You're a collector of witches?"

"Not a collector. A safe space."

"Yeah, I'm sure your Alpha just welcomes everyone with open arms, no strings attached, no ulterior motives, no agenda whatsoever. I'm not buying it. Why would he?" Atlas asked.

"Because his mate is a witch too." I paused to let that sink in. "She was marked for death at the age of four and her parents escaped with her, though she was a triplet and her sisters were executed. They were just babies. Kyle would never do that to anyone. We're wolves. We protect people. That's what we do. And as you can imagine, this pack is a bit overly protective of witches. I mean, our Pack Mother is one of the strongest witches I know."

"Oh yeah, what's her power?" Ned asked.

"She's a natural Alpha but also can heal and control the elements."

"Shit, you have a true Alpha she-wolf here?"

"Yes, we do."

"But that's batshit crazy. They're dangerous."

"Damn right she is."

"You're proud of this?"

"Extremely."

"But why?"

"Doesn't matter," Atlas said. "I smell bullshit here. No witch has more than one power."

I grinned back at him through the mirror. "Oh, she wasn't born with three. I told you; she was a triplet. Was. When her sisters died, she acquired their powers as well."

"That's not possible."

"Tell me that after you meet her."

"We're going to meet her?" Ned asked.

"I'll be surprised if she isn't already waiting at headquarters for our arrival. Kelsey likes to welcome every new witch to the territory. It's sort of personal for her, as you can imagine."

Without another word, I pulled into the parking lot at the Lodge.

"What is this place?" Ned asked.

"It's a resort. The Lodge brings in a lot of people to this territory."

"Humans?"

"Sometimes. Not so much lately. After a few massive rescue missions, we're using up a lot of the space here. But don't worry. There's still plenty of rooms left for all of you." I turned to Mirage. "But not you."

"What? Why not me?"

Before I could answer her, Atlas chimed in with a smirk on his face. "Because you already have an actual house just up the street with lover boy here, remember?"

# Mirage

## Chapter 20

My cheeks heated at whatever Atlas was insinuating. I certainly wasn't going to ask him to clarify it.

"Leave her alone. We haven't exactly had time to discuss next steps for us yet," Colin surprised me by saying. "Now come on, and let's get this over with."

Over with? Like this is the end? I suddenly realized I didn't want this to end. Whatever this was between us, it felt good and right. I wasn't ready to let that go.

I sat there frozen as Atlas and Ned got out and ran off to catch up with the others. But Colin just walked around and opened the door for me, holding out his hand, and waiting for me to accept it.

When I did, he pulled me out of the vehicle and then pressed my back up against the side of it.

"Listen. I know we really need to talk, and I don't want to overwhelm you or press you to make any decisions right now. If you'd rather stay here at the Lodge with everyone else, that's fine. But if you'd rather go home, you're automatically granted permission while we're mating."

"By home, you mean your home?"

He growled, but it didn't rattle my inner wolf in the least.

"It ceased to be just my home the second I met you. What's mine is yours. That's our home now. And maybe you want to find the family you were taken from all those years ago. If you can give me any details or a pack name, I can find them, well Archie can find them. He can find anyone. If that's what you need, okay. But just remember, I'm your family now too."

I stared at him in shock. He couldn't possibly know how powerful those words were to me.

Family?

I had a family.

He was my family.

*Mine*, my wolf agreed.

"I don't remember much about my family, Colin. Vague images at best. I couldn't even begin to tell you what part of the world I'm from. I was eight years old and traumatized by a lot of things that happened. Aside from a few random blips in time, I don't recall much before my first collection, and most of that I'd honestly rather forget."

"If that ever changes, the pre-taken part, not the rest, and you remember anything that we can connect back to your past, I'll make certain you get back there. Preferably for a visit though, unless you really need to move there."

I stared at him curiously. "And what if I did need to move there?"

"Then I hope to God you want company, because I'd follow you anywhere."

His lips crushed against mine. He had kissed me twice before. I'd lost it the first time but had been so freaked out already the second time that it had actually calmed me. We'd already had sex, how could kissing hurt at this point?

I'd felt so naïve when he explained what we'd done. No, what I'd done. But he hadn't made me feel bad or insecure about it in any way. He'd been sweet and kind about everything. I didn't feel self-conscious about it or even have any regrets about what we'd done. It had felt like the most natural thing in the world, and so did kissing him now as I sighed and gave in to the sensations he was creating in me.

When I started to kiss him back, he slowed things down and smiled against my lips. Pulling away with one last peck, he was grinning like a fool.

"Better," he said.

"I didn't mean to freak you out. I don't even know where to begin to find my family because it was so long ago. I was only speaking hypothetically."

"I know. We really have a lot to talk about and figure out. There hasn't exactly been much time for that with everything going on, but things should start to settle down some now." He reached for my hand linking our fingers together. "Come on. They'll be waiting for us."

"Where did Atlas and the others go?"

He chuckled. "Inside to give us a little privacy."

I scrunched up my nose. "Is there even such a thing around here?"

Instinctively I looked up to see a camera next to the door. My whole demeanor changed. This wasn't any different than any other place I'd been. Maybe more time outside, but still always being watched.

"What just happened?" Colin asked.

I pointed up. "They're watching us."

He started to relax. "Oh. Is that all?"

"Is that all? I've been watched and monitored practically my whole life. How is this place any different? You said we'd be free here."

I felt betrayed, and it hurt like a bitch.

"Babe, calm down." He looked around and then lowered his voice. "This is a top secret, highly secured building. Of course there are going to be cameras everywhere. But that's here. That's not at our house and only in a few areas around town for monitoring and Pack safety. I can show you where they all are if it will make you feel better."

I considered what he said and slowly nodded. It made sense but still creeped me out, feeling so exposed outdoors like this.

Sadly, once we were inside, and went down an elevator and into the basement through a steel encased door, I started to relax. It felt more normal than outdoors. I hated thinking like that, but it was the truth. No windows, no sign of night or day. This was my life and what I'd expected to see since Colin first walked into my life.

Still, this place was very different than any collection I'd ever lived in. For starters, there were computers everywhere and people working and running around. I felt like I was just in everyone's way. I couldn't quite get the flow down. It made me feel off my game.

Colin wrapped an arm around me and escorted me down the hall to a room with way too many people for my comfort. It was standing room only, though one open chair remained.

I was certain I'd never seen the man at the head of the table before, or the one beside him. A few of the others looked vaguely familiar.

"Hello. You must be Mirage. Please take a seat," he said.

There was something in his voice that made me want to jump at his bidding. It was terrifying. Who was he?

I dared a glance up at Colin, but he just smiled and nodded, signifying I should obey. I wasn't sure I had a choice in that. It was much like the device on my spine without the pain. So I took a seat without argument.

"Okay, let's get started. I'm Kyle Westin. I'm not sure if you've met everyone, so please go around the room and give your names."

"Silas."

"Painter."

"Michael."

Atlas was sitting next to him and looked around and then shrugged. "Atlas."

"Cypress."

"Grant."

"Taylor."

"Tucker."

"Ben."

"Boris."

"Gwen."

"Ramona."

"Hi, I'm Ned."

"Magnolia," she said rolling her eyes at Ned.

"Tarron."

"Jake."

"Lachlan."

"Walker."

"Mirage," I said when my turn came as I tried to commit all these names to memory.

"Colin."

"Baine."

"Linc."

"And I'm Patrick," the redheaded man next to Kyle said in a deep accent. "Welcome to San Marco, home of Westin Pack. We apologize for the unusual activity post rescue. That was not our usual procedure. I'll be looking into the circumstances that led to this whole mess."

"It's simple really. I found my mate," Colin said.

My jaw dropped. It wasn't like it was a surprise to most of the people in the room, but the two up front were strangers and clearly people of authority.

Kyle grinned. "I had heard congratulations were in order."

"In the chaos of the moment, we hadn't considered he had implanted trackers," Michael said. "That's my fault. I take full responsibility."

"No, it's not all on him. I should have known better," Tarron insisted.

"Bravo team was taking lead. I'll assume full responsibility," Silas argued.

"Enough," Kyle said. "Mistakes were made. Extenuating circumstances were in play. We get it. It was identified quickly and the situation was rectified, correct?"

"Yes, sir," Michael and Silas replied in unison.

"Good. Then let's move on. Taylor, you insisted on this mission, so go ahead and give us the run down."

"Yes, sir." She went into the story of how they had come to rescue us. Apparently, it had all been at her insistence after she saw me at the auction. I had no idea and felt bad about questioning her intentions.

Next, she told them about how we'd rushed home after Colin revealed he'd found his mate and how I'd alerted them to the trackers the next morning.

Finally, she recounted our adventures around the world and how the Collector had chased us until the chips were removed and implanted into a bunch of pigs.

"That sounds like quite the adventure," Patrick said.

Baine started to laugh. "Pigs? You put the trackers in pigs?"

"I did," Grant confessed with a grin. "He could be looking for them for a while, or he's stuck on that ship for the next month. Either way, we shouldn't have to worry about him anymore."

"Still, I'd like to request my team be grounded for at least the next three months as we tighten our borders proactively. We've thrown him off for now, but once he does realize what happened, it's not far-fetched to think he could backtrack, starting here."

"I agree," Patrick said. "Delta team will be grounded for the next three months. Bravo, continue chasing leads on the Collectors we've identified to date."

"Great. So, to our guests, we'd like to invite you all to stay as long as you need. Patrick will see to your accommodations here at the Lodge and you temporarily have permission to move about my territory."

"Temporarily?" Ned asked.

"I knew they wouldn't accept a fox and a bear into wolf territory," Atlas said.

"Hey now, bear, fox," Baine said pointing to himself and then to Tarron. "This is just preliminary as we start a process of questioning and helping you decide what comes next for you and where you'd like to go."

"I do accept transfers here, but there is a process for that as well," Kyle explained. "And I do not discriminate against other species. If you have any trouble at all here, you let me know and I'll handle it."

The door opened and a beautiful woman walked in.

"Sorry I'm late. I already had a morning commitment over at the school."

"You're just in time," Kyle said as he grabbed her around the waist, pulling her towards him and kissing her in front of everyone.

I looked around the room wondering if anyone else thought it was weird and inappropriate. No one seemed bothered by it though.

"Everyone, this is my gorgeous mate, Kelsey."

She blushed.

The others began to whisper. Not the Westin Force guys, but my friends.

"Did you say Kelsey?" Atlas asked.

Suddenly it dawned on me who she was, and I gasped.

"Yes," she confirmed.

"The witch with three powers?"

"The one and only," her mate said.

It was the oddest thing to me. He was actually proud of that fact. There was no doubt in my mind about that. He was practically beaming with it. I'd never in my life seen anyone but a Collector get that excited about a witch. Others feared us. It left a terrible feeling in the pit of my stomach.

Colin leaned down and whispered in my ear. "What's wrong?"

I shook my head. Now wasn't the time to explain it.

"No offense, but we're all a little skeptical," Atlas said as he continued talking on behalf of all of us. "Can we see?"

Kelsey just smiled. "A curious lot. Of course. I have no secrets here and trust me, it's the most refreshing thing in the world."

She opened her hand and blew into the palm of it. Suddenly there was a small tornado there. She moved her hand around and then set it free to dance across the table.

"So the power of wind is one."

"Actually it's not that. I have elemental powers," she explained.

"Huh?"

Next she called to the water in her mate's glass sitting on the table and it came to her.

"So wind and water."

"I can manipulate them," she told us. "Not create them. It works for fire and earth as well. I'm also a healer."

"And you really do not want to sample her fecking manipulation powers. They are tied to her Alpha powers. She could command an army at her will if she chose," Patrick explained.

"Which I would never do on purpose," Kelsey insisted.

"Which is why we'd all follow you to the ends of the Earth," Baine said causing the others to chuckle.

Kelsey blushed again.

"I've seen the elemental powers. I need to see another. Maybe healing?" Atlas insisted.

I wanted to stomp on his foot and tell him to shut up already. We'd seen enough. She was obviously a very powerful witch.

"Oh, oh," Ned said jumping up and pulling off his shirt. "I scratched my side when we were getting off that ship. It's nothing serious, but would it work?"

Kelsey looked around the room and smiled. "Sure."

Walking over, she laid her hand over the scratch. "There."

When she pulled her hand away there wasn't even the slightest sight of the scratch.

"Wow. This is insane," Atlas blurted out.

"Happy now?" Gwen asked rolling her eyes.

"Okay, so next, we're going to take each of you individually into a room for just some quick questions. You are free to answer them or not. That's totally up to you. I know it's been a long day and you may be asked to come back a few times over the next several days. Your answers are all voluntary and used to help us save as many others as possible. Now that you've all met Kelsey you'll be seeing more of her as well. She likes to take a personal part in onboarding new witches, for obvious reasons," Kyle said.

"Wait, there are more?" Cypress interrupted.

Kelsey nodded. "We have several who choose sanctuary here. A few of our younger witches are currently away at college, but they'll be back during their holiday breaks."

That didn't make any sense to me. I was convinced that Kyle Westin was a Collector. But why would he let part of his collection go off to college like that? I hadn't really believed for a second that they would really allow any of us to leave, but now I was just confused and not sure what to think.

# Colin

## Chapter 21

I was extremely relieved when Mirage got out of her debriefing. They wouldn't let me go in with her, and it had set my wolf on edge. I'd taken to pacing the hallway outside the room I knew they had her in.

Relief flooded me as the door finally opened and she walked out.

Lachlan nodded to me and smiled. "Thank you for talking with us, Mirage."

"Sure," she said before turning to me. "They said I could stay here with the others or go home with you. Can we go home now?"

*Home.* She wanted to go home. My face hurt from grinning so hard.

"Let's go home."

We only stopped briefly to say goodnight to the others and let them know that she had chosen not to stay at the Lodge. I promised them we'd see them again tomorrow.

Mirage looked exhausted, but I didn't say anything. I probably looked like a wreck too.

We were quiet on the ride home, but when she sighed contentedly as the house came into view, I thought just maybe everything was going to work out okay.

After we parked and got out to stretch, she followed me into the house.

"Do you want something to eat?" I asked her.

She frowned. "No one's ever really asked me that before. I just get served food on a schedule. I'm so tired, I don't even care if I eat right now."

"It has definitely been a long day. Think you can stay up long enough to run out for pizza?"

Her jaw dropped. "Pizza?"

"Yeah. We've got a great place in town. We can go there, or I can call in an order for delivery, but pickup might be faster. I could give you a quick tour of town if you'd like."

"Okay. I probably shouldn't fall asleep this early anyway."

The sun was still out and hadn't quite begun to set yet.

"Great. What do you want?"

"Huh?"

"On your pizza, babe. What do you want on your pizza?"

Her mouth opened to respond and then shut at least three times before her shoulders finally sagged.

"I don't know. I've never had pizza before."

"What?"

She huffed and glared at me. "I've never had pizza, okay?"

"Never."

She shook her head.

"Do you know what pizza is?"

"I'm not a complete moron, Colin. I've seen pizza in movies."

"Okay, okay. No need to get defensive. In that case, we'll start with the basics."

I picked up the phone and hit the number I had on speed dial for just such emergencies.

"Hey Colin, what are you having today?"

I chuckled. "I'm going to mix things up a bit today. Let's go with a small cheese, a small pepperoni, a small supreme, and a medium meat lovers."

"Dang man, smalls? What's that?" he teased.

"You heard me."

"Alright, alright. You got it. Having a small party tonight or something?"

"Or something."

"Give us about twenty minutes."

"Great. Thanks, man." I turned back to Mirage who was studying me closely. I wished I knew what she was thinking. "Ready?"

"Um, yeah."

As we left the house, I took a detour to drive by the Alpha house and Westin Foundation before driving her through town on our little tour. I pointed out everything along the way and she seemed captivated by it all.

"It looks like the kind of place you'd see in a movie. I didn't even know such a place was real."

"It's real, sweetheart."

Pulling up in front of Pino's, I asked if she wanted to come in, but she declined. I could sense her curiosity but also her hesitation. I tried to imagine things from her perspective. It was hard to imagine her growing up in a six-by-six cell like the one I'd found her in. The fact that I'd heard her and the others say that was the nicest place they'd ever lived truly broke my heart.

How would it feel to see the world through her eyes? Had she been allowed to go to school? I suspected the answer was no. Could she even read or write? There were still so many things I needed answers to.

But for tonight, I was selfishly just going to enjoy some alone time with her at last.

"Hey Colin. Welcome back. Dad didn't tell me you were coming home today," Kevin said.

"Yeah, we're all back. Got in this morning."

He shrugged. "I had football practice after school and then came straight to work. So I really haven't seen him today. Is, um, everyone okay?"

The pain his question caused hit me right in the gut.

"Yeah, everyone's fine."

Relief radiated from him. "That's great. Well, here's your pizzas. Have a great night."

He ran off to tell his boss the news. It was always a big deal when a team returned, especially Delta because we were closer to the Pack than the other units.

I stood there trying to get a handle on my emotions. No kid should have to worry about whether his dad, or his unit, was coming back in one piece or not. This was all my fault. If I'd been paying closer attention, Linc wouldn't have had to save me, getting shot in the process.

No sooner did I think the thought, the door opened and Linc walked in with Christine. They were smiling and laughing.

"Hey, welcome home," Christine said when she saw me standing there. She threw her arms around my neck and hugged me.

A menacing growl sounded from behind her. We both turned to look in time to see Mirage furious and shaking before turning and running from the building.

"So, that would be Mirage, Colin's mate I was telling you about."

"Congratulations by the way. I am so excited to meet her. Are you taking those pizzas to go?"

"Yeah. It's been a crazy day. Week? Hell if I even know how long we were gone. It was a long one. We're just going to head home and eat and then crash."

"Go grab our pizza," she said to Linc.

"What are you up to?" he asked her.

"Just do it."

As soon as he walked away, she turned on me. "I have no doubt that after all of that and being surrounded by several unmated males that all you want to do is shack up and stake your claim."

"Chris!" Linc warned her suddenly standing there with two large pizzas in hand.

I looked at my stack of mostly smalls and then back to his.

"You each get your own pizza?" I asked.

"We couldn't agree on toppings, plus I like the leftovers to take for lunch. But you're changing the subject. Can we please come over and meet her. Just to eat and then we'll be off."

I groaned. This was my chance to have her all to myself.

"Tonight? We just got back."

"Please?"

"I'm sorry, Colin. When she sets her mind to something, it's really hard to change it."

"Fine. But only for an hour."

"Perfect," Christine said with a grin that didn't make me feel great about my decision.

They walked out with me, and I was relieved to find Mirage back in the car. She looked furious.

"Hey, it's okay. I'm sorry that upset you. Chris is mated. She's just a friend. That's Linc's mate. He's on my team, remember? We're all like family around here," I tried to explain. "She was just happy I was home."

I realized that the distraction had broken me out of the state of depression I'd been nose-diving towards since Kevin's relief over everyone's safe return. I'd been there a thousand times since that day. If I closed my eyes, I could still see his face and determination as Linc knocked me out of the way and took that bullet in my place.

But I didn't go there this time. Christine and Linc's sudden appearance and then Mirage's reaction to her hugging me had kept me from spiraling.

Mirage had her arms crossed over her chest and was fuming with anger. I reached out to calm her, but she brushed me off.

Sighing, I silently drove off toward home.

By the time we arrived, her fists were clenched, and her face was scrunched up.

"Babe. I'm telling you, it was nothing."

"I don't know what's wrong with me," she told me. "I can't control it."

"Control what?"

"Her," she whispered.

Mirage jumped from the car just as three more pulled up. She looked a little crazy... no, wild.

As Christine jumped out to say hello and introduce herself, Mirage growled a deep and guttural sound.

"Stay back," I warned.

The others started gathering around and I realized it wasn't just Chris and Linc, but Michael and Callie were there, and surprisingly, so was Tucker and Annie. The mates of Delta were coming to welcome mine to our little pack.

I would have been a bit overwhelmed by the reality of it if we weren't in an all-out crisis.

Annie looked at her disagreeably. "What's wrong with her?"

"Annie," Tucker admonished.

"I'm serious. Is she rabid or something?"

The others glared at her. "What? I'm not risking catching something."

"She's not rabid," I snapped.

"Sweetheart, look at me. I need to you to calm down."

Mirage shook her head. "I don't know what's happening. I can't stop her."

I relaxed and smiled. "So don't."

"What? Are you insane?" she yelled.

Her breathing was becoming ragged, and I could feel how scared she was.

"What's going on?" I heard Callie ask.

"She's never shifted before," I explained.

"Never?" Annie asked. "Is she some sort of freak?"

I growled at her. Normally Tucker would step in and intervene for her, but he didn't this time.

"Are you going to just let him get away with that?"

"Yeah, I am. You're being a bitch and need to stop."

My jaw dropped as I whipped around to look at him. I had never heard him stand up to her like that. Normally he just took whatever she dished out and often even defended her for it, especially in her presence.

Callie slowly approached keeping a safe distance from me.

"Hi, Mirage. I'm Callie, Michael's mate." Her voice was calm, almost soothing when she spoke, and her hands were outstretched as if she were approaching a stray dog for the first time. In a way, I supposed it was kind of similar. "I understand you've never shifted before. I've helped plenty of people through this process before. Trust me, this is the most natural thing in the world."

She shook her head. "It's not s-s-safe," she managed stutter out.

"She's been repressing her wolf for years, hasn't she?"

"I suspect so."

Michael stepped up to his mate. "You're safe here," he told her. "Colin will protect you and we'll protect him. That's what we do around here. We watch out for each other."

"It's going to be okay," Tucker added as he stepped up next to Michael, though Annie didn't join us.

"Stop fighting her, sweetheart. Just let it happen. It's the most freeing feeling in the world."

Her head quirked towards me.

"You should show her. Your wolf could call hers out," Tucker suggested.

"That's actually a good idea," Callie agreed.

"Hey, you sound like that's a rare thing."

Callie just looked at him causing Michael to snort.

I began taking my clothes off, but that seemed to make Mirage even more freaked out as her head whipped around towards each of them.

Christine laughed. "Don't be an idiot. Just shift. She's not going to tolerate you naked in front of anyone in this state."

"She's right," Linc agreed. "Not the first set of clothes you've lost and won't be the last."

I looked down and sighed. I loved these jeans. But this was more important. Clothing could be replaced. My mate could not. Without further hesitation, I shifted.

Mirage startled and gasped in surprise.

I approached her slowly despite my wolf's excitement to finally meet our mate.

She stared down at me in awe.

"Don't fight it," Callie said. "Just take a deep breath and let the shift happen."

She shook her head.

"You can do this," Christine encouraged her.

I sat back on my hind legs and howled. My wolf was calling to hers.

Even as she continued to protest, her wolf overpowered her. Clothes flew in all directions towards me as her wolf literally exploded from her.

Standing before me was a gorgeous light gray wolf. She was similar in color to me, only my wolf was darker. She was beautiful, the prettiest wolf I'd ever seen.

My wolf howled once more as he danced around in circles excitedly.

# Mirage

## Chapter 22

I stood there in shock.

I did it!

I was in my fur. I couldn't believe it.

"Way to go, Mirage!" the woman that had been hugging Colin at the pizza place cheered.

I refrained from growling at her this time, distracted by the excitement of this new experience but still hyper alert to my surroundings. I hated that so many people had witnessed my first shift, but they all seemed supportive and encouraging.

"We should leave them," Michael said.

"No. We should all shift and join them for a run," Callie insisted.

"I'm not doing that. I already took my shower tonight. I'm going home. Come on Tucker."

"No, Callie's right. We need to be supportive and show Mirage that she's part of the team."

"Tucker, get in the car."

"No," he said again, tossing her the keys. "Go if you must, but this is important. She's been living in captivity for twenty years.

She was just a kid when they took her. She needs a strong support system to see her through this. I'm staying and you should too."

"That's not happening. Get your own ride home."

Annie turned and stomped off, got in the car, and drove away.

I growled as she went.

"Don't bother," Tucker told me.

I hated how sad he looked, but also determined.

No one said a thing about it as they started stripping.

"How did you know all that about her?" Linc asked.

"She was in my room for assessments today and shared it with us. I probably shouldn't have blurted that out like that."

"It's okay," Michael told him. "She's family."

Family? Me? Why would they feel that way? They didn't even know me.

"Annie's family too, and we haven't given up on her yet," Christine told him.

"I know. And I'll have hell to pay later for this, but some things are just too important not to stand up to her on. My problem. I'll deal with it later. Don't worry. She's just been in a mood since our last assignment. We'll be okay."

Both couples shared a silent look, but none of them said anything more as one by one they started to strip out of their clothes.

Colin's wolf approached and rubbed up against me. The close contact startled me and shot tingles through my body. I turned to look at him. His wolf was larger than mine, but he was a beautiful gray wolf. I realized I had no idea what color my wolf was, but when I turned to look, I just went in a circle. I could see my tail though. It was a lighter color but tipped in gray.

When Colin chuffed and bounced around happily, I realized I was just chasing my tail.

I wanted to groan in embarrassment.

That's when it dawned on me that I was in my wolf form, but I was also still me. She had always felt like a second entity with a mind of her own. I had imagined that shifting would feel like losing myself to her, but that wasn't the case at all. We were both still here, coexisting as always, just in a different form.

It was so odd trying to think about it, but it just felt natural.

Michael's wolf barked and captured my attention. I realized then that the others had shifted too. There were now five additional wolves surrounding me. I should have felt trapped and uncomfortable, but I didn't. I felt whole like I was a part of something bigger than me. I didn't know if that was just because of Colin or if it was all of them.

They called me family, pack. I'd never let myself really imagine having that again. Instead, I'd made my own family at each collection I'd been in only to have them ripped away from me each time I was sold off to the next highest bidder.

This felt different. This felt like forever.

Michael barked again as he took off running around the corner of the house. The others followed, all except Colin, who hung back waiting for me to join them.

His big head nodded towards them, and there was something so human about the motion that I knew without a doubt that it was my Colin communicating with me. He was consciously there too.

I nodded and turned to run, only to stumble.

He chuffed, sounding like a weird laugh.

I snapped at him for it, but he licked my face, and I instantly forgave him.

Concentrating this time, I took a solid step and then another and another until I was running to catch up with the others as Colin followed right on my flank.

The wind blew through my fur as I picked up speed. Callie had been right. This was the most free I'd ever felt.

Michael led us into the woods and down to a creek where we splashed and played until the sun set and he barked for us to return.

I didn't want to leave. I wasn't ready to return to the real world that I didn't even fully understand. But when Colin barked at me and then ran behind me and nudged me with his head, I finally conceded, praying the whole way that I would be allowed to shift again soon. I was so ready to fully explore this side of me.

Back at the house the others shifted and redressed. It dawned on me that I didn't have any clothes to change into now because I'd shredded them on my shift.

Colin stood at the door and barked until Tucker ran over and opened it. He motioned to me with his head to follow and even let me walk in ahead of him. At the last second, he turned back and barked at Linc.

"Yeah, fine. I'll grab your pizza."

I had no idea how he had known what was being asked. It was weird, but Colin seemed satisfied and trotted into the house and down the hall to his bedroom. *Our bedroom*, I thought.

It took me a few minutes, maybe longer, to figure out how to shift back into my skin. It wasn't until Colin shifted and stood there completely naked talking to me that my wolf retreated and allowed me to shift.

I stood up, looking him up and down. The first time we'd had sex I'd been going on pure instinct with no idea of what I was doing—what we were doing. This time, I knew exactly what it was and what I wanted.

Walking to him, I wrapped my arms around his neck and kissed him, really kissed him this time. I wanted to feel everything he had to offer, starting with this kiss.

When I sighed softly and my lips parted against his, his tongue slipped into my mouth. It was an odd sensation that excited me in new ways. Cautiously, I let my tongue swirl with his as I smiled against his lips. I couldn't remember why on Earth I had ever thought kissing him was a bad idea.

His kisses melted away all the bad memories and fears I'd had about intimacy. I craved contact with him as I pressed myself even closer to him.

"Sometimes it takes time to shift back. Do you need any help in there?" Callie yelled out.

Our kisses never faltered as he moaned, and I felt him growing hard between us. I was eager for more and may have growled a little.

Michael chuckled somewhere off in the distance.

"I think he's got this under control. And this little welcome party is officially over. We'll try again another time."

"Are you sure?" she asked.

Colin's hands found the swell of my butt, and he gently lifted me up as I wrapped my legs around his waist and grinded myself against him causing a loud moan to escape me.

"Yup, I'm sure. They're going to be busy for a while. Let's give them some privacy."

The front door opened and closed followed soon by car doors and the sound of retreating tires.

"Alone at last," Colin whispered against my mouth, tickling my lips and making me giggle. "I want to devour every inch of you, but if you get unsure or uncomfortable, you just have to let me know and I'll stop."

I nodded. "I trust you," I whispered.

Those words were terrifying, but true. I had never trusted anyone in my life as much as I trusted Colin.

When his mouth left mine, I started to pout but then felt a few kisses across my cheek, and then he was nibbling lightly on my earlobe. It sent a whole new kind of sensation through me. Next, he trailed kisses and little bites down my neck and across my shoulder, stopping to focus on one spot in particular that made my canines elongate into sharp points.

I gasped and pulled back to show him.

"Soon," he told me, blowing on the spot on my neck and then sucking it into his mouth as he carried me to the bed and gently laid me down as he remained standing with my legs still wrapped around him.

"I want you inside me again," I told him.

He smirked. "I'm getting there. Have a little patience."

Before I could protest, he reached out and cupped my breasts in each hand.

I gasped in surprise as the pad of his thumbs circled my nipples and sent shockwaves of pleasure straight to my core.

He leaned down and licked the trail his thumb had made on one side. And when he sucked one hard nipple into his mouth and lightly grazed it with his teeth, my legs tightened around his waist pulling him right against my core.

"Yes," I cried out, encouraging him and relishing in this feeling he was creating within me as I rubbed myself against him, making him even harder.

It didn't last long though before he stepped back and broke my hold on his waist as he kissed his way down my body. I was nearly blind with overwhelming sensations when he lowered his mouth to my core, and I bucked against him in shock.

He was licking, kissing, and sucking in places I never dreamed I'd ever be touched and didn't know anyone did this. Still, I craved more.

My hands fisted in his hair, and I pressed myself into his face, showing him what I needed when I didn't have the words.

It was such a new experience and nothing at all like when we'd had sex. When his tongue pierced me, I cried out.

I could feel him smiling against me as he found one particular spot and started sucking hard just as his fingers replaced the spot his tongue had just been. The combination was more than I could bear as my senses overloaded.

Just like when I'd had sex with him, my body became uncomfortably tight, and then it was like everything within me broke free and exploded, causing my whole body to shake violently as I cried out his name.

"Colin!"

Grinning like a fool, he climbed onto the bed with me. My body felt like putty in his hands as he moved us to the center of the bed and climbed over me. His knees nudged my legs wider, and before I could even come down from the high he'd just caused, he was pushing inside me.

I thought my body would go into shock at that point and completely short-circuit, but then he leaned down and kissed me.

Greedily, I kissed him back as he pressed into me, pulled back, and did it again and again until we had a steady rhythm going, though our kisses lacked the same control. My arms wrapped around his back and my nails scrapped against his skin.

He moaned loudly followed by a little growl that excited me and pushed my body to the breaking point once more.

"Colin! Colin!" I cried out as my body shattered into a million pieces, pulling him along with me as he moaned out my name before collapsing on top of me.

I didn't even mind the extra weight. It felt amazing being that close to him and knowing that he'd felt as good as I had.

After a minute or two, he rolled off and wrapped me up in his arms. I laid my head on his shoulder and fell fast asleep.

# Colin

## Chapter 23

I wasn't given any time off to just be with my mate, which was frustrating. While he apologized for it, Michael had called me in to work the very next day.

"I know Colin and Lachlan are returning from the field and normally would get a few days off, especially you, Colin, having found your mate. But after the potential of a breach surfaced with the witches we rescued wearing tracking devices to potentially lead a Collector right here, Kyle's a bit on edge. And when Kyle is worried, Patrick is worried. He's really pressing in on us to get those new volunteers trained as well as upping border security. Sorry Colin, but this is your area of expertise. I really need you on this."

"It's fine. I'll get with Lane and set up classes. We were already in the process of working on it before we got shipped out. It shouldn't take long to regroup and get everything in place. I'll head over there as soon as we adjourn."

"Thanks man. We all owe you for this one."

"How's Mirage doing, settling in?"

"Fine, I hope. She was still out cold when I left."

"You didn't tell her you were leaving?" Lachlan asked.

I shrugged. "I left her a note."

"Can she even read?" Tucker blurted out.

I growled back at him. What were they playing at?

"That wasn't meant to be disrespectful, but Colin, she was eight when they first took her. For the last twenty years she has been traded around to more collections than we even want to consider exist. I'm just saying, it's highly unlikely any of them sent her off to school."

It wasn't something I hadn't considered already. I just hadn't asked her and this morning I wasn't really thinking as I packed up to come in after Michael's call.

"I don't know," I told him honestly.

"Before you meet up with Lane, stop by your house and check on your mate. If there's any trouble, just let me know."

"Callie's working today but I'm sure she can swing a few well-checks and stop by to see her."

"Thanks," I muttered.

"And Christine is in the office today, but Liam took the day off, so if need be, I'm sure she'd be happy to work remotely and hang out with Mirage today," Linc said.

Ever since he found his mate he has started talking more, and it was still a bit weird to get used to.

"Um, yeah, thanks. That would be great."

"She's been excited to meet her."

I smiled and nodded.

"Well, I'd volunteer Annie for it, but with the mood she's been in lately, she'd just say no. You guys don't need our drama in your life right now anyway," Tucker said.

The room got awkwardly quiet.

"So we have a plan then," Walker said, breaking the silence like it was never there.

"Yeah, Colin, you'll take care of new volunteers. Linc and Walker tag team current volunteer checks. And Tucker and Lachlan, get in your fur and give me a full perimeter check."

"Yes, sir," they all said as he dismissed us.

"Michael, if it's okay with you, I'm going to swing by and check on Mirage before heading over to see Lane, but I'll call him on the way to get things rolling."

"Sounds good."

I couldn't wait to get home to see my mate. Even knowing I couldn't stay, it didn't matter. I'd take every second I could with her. I sped the whole way there.

I expected to find her at home exploring the house or something. But it didn't look like she'd even woken up yet. I started to panic as I ran down the hall and opened the bedroom door.

The bed was neatly made, and Mirage was sitting on the chair in the corner of my room with the remote in her hand. When I walked in without knocking, she jumped and tossed the remote away like it had just burnt her.

Relief shone on her face as she got up and ran into my arms.

"Hey, it's okay. What's wrong?"

"No one came. I waited, but no one came."

"Came for what?" I asked.

"Came with breakfast." She lowered her voice to a whisper. "I'm hungry."

"Babe, there's food in the kitchen."

She looked at me blankly and then nodded. "Okay. I didn't know."

She walked away and down the hall looking a little anxious. When she reached the kitchen, she sat down at the table looking around, confused.

"Where's the food?"

"Excuse me?"

"You said there was food in the kitchen. I don't see any."

I walked over to the refrigerator and opened it. "Food." Then I went to the pantry and opened it along with three cabinets. "Food, food, and more food. You're not going to starve. There's still all the pizza we got last night. You can toss it into the oven and heat it up if you want. It'll taste just as fresh as it would have last night."

I suddenly felt like an ass for not remembering we hadn't eaten dinner. I'd grabbed a donut from the break room at headquarters, but if I was honest, I was a little hungry too.

"Here, I'll put it on for us. Do you want something to drink?"

She blushed. "I drank some water from the bathroom sink."

"You didn't leave the bedroom?"

"Of course not."

"Why?"

She looked at me like I was insane.

"You didn't tell me I could," she blurted out. "And I don't know how to toss pizza into an oven. I've never even had pizza. The kitchen is strictly off limits. Only consume food that is given to you. Nothing else. Sharing with others is forbidden."

"What are you talking about?"

"Rules, Colin. Those are the rules."

My stomach churned and I wanted to throw up as her words began to sink in.

"Those rules do not apply here. How many times do I have to tell you this? What's mine is yours now. You can go explore anything in this house. I don't want any secrets from you. Go outside and go for a run if you want. You can walk into town from here, or I'll leave you Christine and Callie's numbers and you can call them. They'd be happy to take you into town. You are free to do whatever you want. If you don't want to sleep in my bed, there are four other rooms for you to choose here. If you want to watch TV all day and veg, do it. Tonight, I'll show you how to use the movie apps too."

"I can pick what I want to watch?" she asked hesitantly, and it broke my heart.

"Yes, you can. You can do absolutely anything, Mirage."

As I tossed the pizza into the oven, something dawned on me, and I ran to grab my phone and quickly dialed Michael's number.

"Hey, everything okay?"

"I'm not so sure. Has anyone checked on our other guests today?"

"I don't think so, why?"

"We may have a problem. You should send someone up to their rooms."

"Talk to me."

"I came home and found Mirage still in our bedroom. She had cleaned up and was feeling guilty for watching television without permission."

"Permission."

"Yup. And she hadn't eaten since lunch yesterday because we fell asleep after the, uh, run, and didn't eat dinner. She was waiting on someone to bring it to her and tell her it was okay to leave the room."

"Shit. I never even thought of that."

"Yeah, you may need to provide meals and do well-checks on everyone for a while until they adjust. I'm not sure how long the others were in captivity, but I think the concept of freedom is a bit lost on my mate. I'm going to see if Lane can come by here so we can get things moving while I help her some, or at least until Christine can get here."

"It's okay. Focus on your mate and do what you need to do. I can pull Linc over to work with the new volunteer training."

"No, Michael, I'm okay. I can do this."

"You're sure?"

"Positive."

As soon as I hung up with him, I called Lane.

"Hey, you lucky sonofabitch. How's mated life treating you?"

I laughed. "It's been interesting to say the least. Hey, if you have a few minutes, do you think you could come by my house? Michael wants us rolling on the new recruits ASAP, but I really need to be here right now."

I heard him rummaging around on his desk before replying. "You're in luck. My schedule is wide open until two."

"Great. Anytime. I'm here now."

"On my way then."

The buzzer on the oven went off as I ended the call.

"Sweetheart, can you get the pizzas out?"

"What?" she shrieked. "How do I do that? I'm not allowed to touch the oven."

I sighed. "You can touch anything here anytime you want."

She considered that for a moment and then reached out and slid her hand up under my shirt. "Does that include you?"

I laughed. "That always includes me, but if you start that right now, the pizzas will burn."

It wasn't easy walking away, but I did and carefully took out the pizzas and laid them out across the counter.

She sniffed the air. "Mmm. That's the smell from the place you got them. It's the most wonderful thing I've ever smelled. It makes my mouth water. I had to come in last night and see it for myself. I knew I wasn't supposed to get out of the car, but I did anyway just for a glimpse of what was causing that amazing smell." She frowned. "And then I saw you with Christine."

"I told you, she's just a friend, like family. Wolves are big huggers. It happens. If it bothers you that much, I'll keep a distance from others."

"No, it's okay. I just wasn't ready for it, and I didn't know I'd react that way."

"It's not uncommon for mating wolves."

"But you haven't had any issues."

I laughed. "I've had to restrain my wolf on more than one occasion."

"You have?"

"Yeah."

"Really? You're not just saying that?"

"Really. Now here, eat something."

"Thanks."

She took the plate of pizza I offered her and sat down at the table.

I continued watching her as she picked up the hot pizza and blew on it before taking her first bite. Her eyes widened and then rolled back in her head.

"Mmm. This is amazing. It's even better than I imagined."

"That's just basic cheese. I grabbed four kinds for you to sample. It'll take some time before you find what your favorite combination is."

"What's yours?"

I pushed my plate towards her. "Meat lovers. Try it."

She put her slice of cheese down and picked up mine, taking a small bite. Her face lit up and she took another larger one before passing it back to me.

"Good, right?"

"That's delicious," she admitted. "I can't decide which I like more. I'm not picky though. I eat whatever I'm given without complaint. Complaining means no food tomorrow."

My nails bit into the palm of my hands as I made fists under the table and tried not to let her know how much it bothered me that she'd ever had these sorts of rules.

"I left a note on the nightstand this morning. Did you see it?"

"Yes."

"Could you read it, Mirage?"

She gave me an indignant look. "I can read. I'm not completely worthless."

"You aren't worthless at all, regardless of whether you can read or not. You are precious to me. You're the most important person in my life. Haven't you figured that out by now?"

She sighed. "Sorry. I obviously didn't go to school, but in my second, or maybe third, collection, there was an older woman who had been a schoolteacher and she taught me in secret. I can read, write, and even do math."

"That's good. Not that it would have mattered either way, but it's good to know."

My phone rang and I saw Michael's picture flash up.

"Excuse me. I have to take this," I told her as I got up and walked out to the front porch. "Hey, did you check on them."

"Yup, and just as you suspected they were all just sitting in their rooms waiting for food and instructions. What the hell?"

"I don't think they even understand what we mean when we say they're free now. Some of the things Mirage has said just makes my blood boil. I hate that she went through all of that."

"Stop it. No good will come of it."

"I know. What are we going to do with them? Did someone at least teach them how to use room service?"

"I dunno if we thought about that, but good idea. I'll send Walker and Lachie back up to go over that with each of them. How's Mirage?"

"Better now that she's eating something. What am I going to do, Michael?"

"Don't worry. I'll have Callie recruit the Force wives to help out. The Bravo team mates really helped her when she first moved here."

I snorted. "You mean when you kidnapped her and drove halfway across the country to bring her here."

"Shut up. You just flew literally around the world for your mate, remember?"

"I didn't kidnap her."

"I mean, you kind of did. What do you think a rescue like that is?"

I started to refute him, then shut my mouth because just maybe he was right.

He started laughing.

"Shut up. It's not the same," I insisted.

"Keep telling yourself that."

Two police cars pulled up to my house. I gave a quick wave.

"Hey, the cavalry is here. Let me go and get back to work. Thanks for checking on them."

"They aren't solely your responsibility, Colin."

"Kind of feels like it," I said before hanging up on him and turning my attention to Lane instead. "Hey man, thanks for coming by. Come on in." I nodded to the second arrival. "Callie."

"Is Mirage up?"

"Yeah, come on in. We were just eating. There's plenty of pizza if you're hungry."

"Sure, don't mind if I do," Lane said.

Callie pushed by me and made a beeline for my mate. Without hesitation, the two women embraced like old friends. It warmed my heart watching them.

"It's Callie, right?"

"You got it. How are you feeling this morning?"

"Good."

"Come on, we can talk in my office. Let the girls catch up."

Lane followed me back there giving a nod to Mirage along the way.

"She's cute."

"Gorgeous," I corrected. "And no offense, but as an unmated male, I would strongly advise from commenting on her. My wolf isn't handling it very well. Sorry. I wasn't thinking when I invited you over."

"I'm no threat to you or your mate. I'm happy for you."

"I know. It's just a bit hard sometimes."

"I hope someday I'll understand that feeling."

"Me too, buddy." Lane was a great man and deserved his chance at a happily ever after.

"You look... better."

"Most of the time I feel better. It sort of hits me in waves now, sometimes when I'm not expecting it. But I have more to live for now, more on the line, and I'm taking that seriously."

"Because of her?"

I grinned like a loon. "Because of her."

"That's great. Gives me hope that someday just maybe I can let go of a few of my own demons with the help of a good mate."

"They don't just go away, but it doesn't always feel so big and all-consuming either."

"I hear you. Still gives me hope. Now, what's all of this about? You did call me over for a reason, and not just to chat, right? Something about new recruits?"

"The volunteer program we were working on," I corrected. "I don't know how much you've heard about what went down."

"Very little I'm afraid. Just enough to know something did."

"Well, when we got to our mission, I found my mate. It wasn't safe for her to stay there, and I insisted we come back home as quickly as possible. So we did. What I didn't know, and in the chaos of it all no one else thought about either, was that she had a tracking device installed inside her. We rescued eight of them in total and they all had trackers."

"You led the bad guy right here?"

"I didn't know it at the time, but yeah. So as soon as it was brought to our attention, we loaded up onto the plane and flew to another location, and then another, and then another as we bounced around the world trying to throw their Collector off. Along the way we were able to remove all their trackers and avoid crossing paths with their Collector—who hasn't stopped looking for them. He turned around and chased their signal before actually coming here, but if he starts backtracking through everything, he could end up here at any time. So we're upping security, and I need to get the new volunteer program up and running ASAP."

"Wait, did you say their Collector? Like the one you all took down here that was after Kelsey?"

"Exactly like that, only this one is relatively new to the game and had a much smaller collection."

"By collection, you mean witches?"

I nodded.

"Great, so we have even more witches moving in."

"What do you have against witches?"

"Nothing. It's just that they seem to draw drama and danger here."

"Yeah, well, that could happen again, which is why we need that program going now."

"That's not a problem. I have a batch of ten. In your absence I've had them doing all sorts of volunteer work throughout the territory. Pretty sure they think it's part of the program and what they signed on for."

I laughed and shook my head. "When can I meet them?"

"How about tomorrow?"

"Perfect. And I really appreciate you coming by. I was on my way to your office but had some things I needed to resolve here first."

Lane chuckled and shook his head. "Is that what you're calling it?"

His phone rang and he quickly answered it. "Sheriff Stoddard... I see... yeah, I'm on my way now. Thanks."

"Sorry man, but I've gotta run."

"What's going on?"

"Got a call from Nonna this morning worried because she couldn't reach Birdie. Had Jenkins run by for a check."

His face said it all.

I shook my head in disbelief.

"Not Birdie. She's like the matriarch of Westin Pack."

"Oh, sorry. She's fine. She just fell and possibly broke her hip. Somehow in the process she managed to wedge herself between the tub and the toilet and they need help getting her out. Her, Nonna, and Tabitha have kept me on my toes since the second I arrived. Oh the stories I could tell. The whole lot of them are crazy. I'm convinced of it. And she reigns as queen of the crazies."

I grinned. "Don't I know it. Before my grandparents died, you could have counted my grandmother into that crazy mix. I grew up hanging out at Birdie's after school. I am well familiar with her antics."

"Well, if you want to join me, you're welcome to. Apparently, it's quite the sight."

"Mind if Callie hangs out with Mirage?"

"Sure. She's got her phone on her if anything comes up."

I quickly said goodbye to the girls and followed Lane out to his car. It still felt weird riding in the front seat of his cruiser. I had never been a bad kid growing up, but I'd gotten in a bit of trouble now and then. Nothing serious. But enough that the old Sheriff never offered me the front seat, that was for sure.

Birdie lived up in the middle of town in a big, beautiful Victorian house. There were several cars out front when we arrived. Lane and I jumped out as soon as the car came to a stop and ran inside.

At a glance I noticed the tea table set for two. Both cups were only half empty. I shook my head.

"What's the situation?" he asked his deputy.

"I don't know, sir. It doesn't make sense, but we can't seem to pull her out. It doesn't look like she should be wedged that tight, but the fact that she cries out in pain every time we touch her doesn't help. She's been asking for you."

"Me?"

"Yeah, you."

I groaned. "Where is she?"

"Micah's in with her now."

"How often does she call you over here?"

"A few times a week," Lane confessed.

I chuckled. "Want me to handle this?"

"Do you think you can?" he asked.

"I fear we're going to have to take the toilet out to get her free," Jenkins said.

I laughed. "I highly doubt that's necessary."

Lane followed me back but when we walked in and she cried out, "Oh, Sheriff, is that you?" I held my finger to my lips for him to stay quiet.

"Sorry Birdie. It's me, Colin."

She was laid out on the floor, lying on her side with her back turned towards us, naked as the day she was born. It was quite the sight.

"She won't even let me look at her," Micah complained.

I nodded for him to leave us alone while Lane held back at the door watching and learning.

"Colin? What the hell are you doing here? Where's the Sheriff?"

"Wanna tell me how you got in this position?"

"I fell, if you must know."

"Getting out of the shower?"

"Yes, of course."

"Why isn't the tub wet then?"

She hesitated. "I've been down here a while."

"Where's your towel, Birdie?"

"I forgot to grab it if you must know. Now where's that handsome doctor? Oh, it hurts so bad," she wailed, but the voice wasn't quite her usual one.

"What are you up to?"

"Well, I declare, I don't have a clue what you're talking about," she said in the voice of a Southern belle.

I laughed. "Really, because there are two cups of tea still out, which means Nonna knew damn well you were just fine when she called in all concerned for your well-being."

"I don't know what you're talking about, son," she said again in a Southern accent.

"Is that character supposed to be from Gone with Wind or Steel Magnolias? I couldn't tell. I think you're slipping."

"Get out of here, boy. You'll ruin everything. I'm waiting on the Sheriff, if you must know."

She wiggled her way out and sat up to glare at me.

"Oh, Sheriff Stoddard," she said in a high-pitched voice. "I guess your handsome deputy loosened me enough to slide right out."

"Birdie, get off the floor," I told her.

She shot me a look, letting me know there would be hell to pay later, but did as she was told. I didn't particularly enjoy being on her bad side.

"It's a miracle," she announced as she stood up. "Thank you so much for rushing down here to help an old lady," she said slyly. Then she walked right past us, stopping at the door to look back over her shoulder at Lane. "Like what you see, Sheriff?"

I struggled holding back my laugh until she made her grand exit.

"Fancies herself a bit of an actress. She always breaks out into a character when she's lying. It's her biggest tell."

He just stood there in shock. "She did all that, faked a fall and an injury, just to get me over here?"

"That would appear correct. Congratulations. You've obviously got a big fan on your hands."

He still looked distraught as we walked out into the living room and told everyone the situation had been handled.

"Thanks for the assist. I don't even want to think about how that would have played out without you."

I shrugged. "I'll catch hell for it later. She's old, and when she gets together with her friends there's no telling what kind of trouble they'll talk each other into. You might want to have a talk with Nonna about filing false claims. Let her off with a warning this time but tell her she'll be thrown in the clinker if she does it again."

"The clinker?"

"Yup. Tell her those exact words."

I'd love to see the look on her face when he did, too, but I needed to get back home to my mate.

As if he could read my mind, he barked some orders at his deputy to wrap up the call.

"How about I run you home now?"

Before I could respond, Birdie stepped out in a flamboyant long silk robe in bright colors loosely tied at the waist.

"Oh Sheriff, come again soon," she said with a wave.

I laughed and walked over to kiss her cheek.

"Behave, Birdie."

"What fun is that?" she protested. "Don't you be a stranger either. It's good to see you. And I heard a rumor that you found your true mate."

I grinned. "I did."

"Well you best be bringing her over to meet me, you here?"

"Yes ma'am."

As I turned to leave, she smacked me on my ass.

"Behave," I warned her.

Outside I could still hear her laughing.

"She's something," Lane said, shaking his head.

"She's harmless, just old and bored."

"If you say so. I'm convinced that woman could run circles around me."

"Oh, for sure," I teased.

It felt good and normal seeing Birdie up to her old tricks, like I'd been transported back in time to easier, happy days when the weight of the world didn't always feel like it sat on my shoulders.

"What the hell?" I asked, seeing half a dozen cars parked in my yard as we pulled up.

He chuckled. "Do you think Birdie was in cahoots with them? Lured us away so Callie and your mate could throw a party?"

I shook my head and grinned. "That would be something. Are you coming in?"

"Nope. I know these cars, and that is a Westin Force mates party. My guess is they're initiating Mirage into their little gang. I make it a point to try to stay out of Westin Force business, especially when it comes to these ladies."

"I should probably check on them."

"Are you sure about that?"

"We do have work to do."

He looked at his watch. "Your new recruits' team should be arriving in about twenty minutes."

I was torn between going in to check on my mate and running quickly in the opposite direction. Callie was with her, and I trusted her to look after my girl. Besides, it was good for her to make friends with the other mates.

In the end I decided on self-preservation.

"I'll follow you to the station."

# Mirage

## Chapter 24

I wasn't really sure how it had happened. One minute Callie and I were talking and the next there was a room full of women. I was struggling to keep up with all of their names, but everyone seemed really nice.

"This is a bit overwhelming, isn't it?" Olivia asked.

I shrugged. "I've never done anything like this before. I hope Colin doesn't get angry. I didn't have the chance to ask his permission."

"You don't need his permission," Vada insisted. "You are your own independent woman."

I wasn't even sure what that was supposed to mean.

In one corner of the room, a sort of kid corral had been set up. Emma stepped out of it after settling a dispute between two little boys. There were kids everywhere, and I couldn't stop staring at them. It had been rare that a baby was born into a collection, and they were taken pretty quickly to be raised by the Collector. I wasn't used to seeing tiny people like this, and I was fascinated by them.

"It takes time," Emma said.

"What does?"

"Adjusting to the outside."

"Oh, are you a witch too? Did you come from a collection?"

She shook her head. "No, but I was in captivity for a long time before Bravo team rescued me and Painter brought me home."

"I was in captivity for a long time too," Vada admitted.

"You were?"

She nodded. "Don't worry. We've got your back."

My shoulders drooped. "I was captured when I was eight. All I know are the rules of the collection. I don't understand how things work here," I confessed.

"You were eight?" Christine asked with a growl.

I nodded.

"That's awful. I want to take these sonofabitches down for this," Susan said, causing the others to laugh.

"Motherhood has made her quite protective," Callie explained. "Apparently, she used to be super sweet and laid back. I don't see it."

They all laughed, so I did too. I wasn't exactly sure what was so funny though.

"Did you get any leads from what we've provided so far?" Taylor asked Susan.

"A few but nothing concrete yet. I'm following the money trail at the moment."

"Susan works at headquarters. She's a computer whiz. I heard she drove Tarron crazy before he found her. She's quite the hacker," Callie told me.

"Boy did she ever."

Susan shrugged. "Still do, all the time."

"Tarron's your mate?"

She nodded. "Yup, he's all mine."

I tried to place him, but there had been so many new names and faces that I couldn't quite make the match from memory.

Alaina walked into the kitchen and opened the refrigerator, pulling out cans of drinks and tossing them to others.

I gasped. "I'm going to get in so much trouble for this."

"For what?" Emma asked.

"You can't just help yourself to food and drinks."

Even though Colin had said it was okay, it felt like a trap. I didn't trust it.

"Was that one of the rules for you?" she asked.

I nodded, worrying my lip as I thought of the various punishments that would be headed my way. I shuddered thinking about the shockwaves that would wrack my body for disobeying.

"That rule doesn't exist here," she said matter-of-factly. "This is your house. That is your fridge. Now walk over there and get a soda out."

"Soda?" I asked. I knew what it was, but I'd never tried it before.

"Yup, you heard me. Be a rebel and go for it."

I wasn't sure what came over me, but as the girls started chanting my name, I took a deep breath, walked over, and opened that refrigerator. I couldn't believe I was actually doing this, but I grabbed one of the cans like the ones I'd seen Alaina toss to others. I popped the top to cheers all around me. I turned around and held it up in the air before tipping it back and drinking it quickly.

"No!" they all cried.

It was so gross that I ran to the sink and spit it out.

"Ew. I thought soda would taste better."

The room exploded in laughter.

"Sweetie, that wasn't soda. That was beer," Olivia told me.

"Beer?"

"Alcohol," she clarified.

My eyes widened and my cheeks burned. I even screwed up my moment of rebellion.

"Why would anyone drink that stuff?"

That only made them laugh harder.

"Here, try this instead," Alaina said offering me one of the red cans that she was drinking. "This is Coke, soda."

I nodded and hesitantly tasted it. It burned my mouth and tingled, but it didn't taste bad.

"Better?" she asked.

I shrugged. "It's still not great."

She grinned. "I suppose they are both acquired tastes."

I set it down. "I think I'll stick to water."

"I'm starving. How old's this pizza?" Emma asked.

"Colin gave it to me for breakfast."

"I can only spare another half hour before I have to get back to the office," Susan said.

"Same," Taylor said.

"Normally I'd agree, but my boss is out of the office today so I'm good."

"How about burgers at the Crate?" Callie suggested. "Come on, you can ride with me."

I froze and shook my head. "I can't just leave."

They all shared looks that made me feel awful. Why would they pity me when I had more than I ever dreamed possible right here.

"You're coming even if I have to carry you out of here."

"Colin will be mad. I'll get in trouble."

Christine laughed. "Mirage, has Colin ever gotten mad?"

I nodded. I'd seen him angry before, like when my Collector came on the boat after us.

"Let me rephrase, mad at you?"

I considered that for a moment and then shook my head. "No."

"And he won't because he loves you too much. He only wants to see you happy."

I nearly choked.

"What? Colin loves me?"

No one loved me, not really. I wasn't even sure I knew what love was.

"Oh yeah, he has it bad for you," Callie agreed.

"I've never seen him so assertive outside of combat. He'd do absolutely anything for you, including letting you go to lunch with us," Taylor said. "I promise you it will be fine. Do you trust me?"

I shook my head. "No offense, but you did buy witches at an auction."

She sighed. "I thought we already explained that."

I shrugged. They had, but that didn't mean I completely believed it.

"Come on, ride with me. I want to show you something. You guys head on over and place our orders. Just tell Jesse I'll have my usual. What do you want?"

"Me?"

"Yeah, to eat. Want do you want to eat?"

I frowned. "No one's ever really asked me that before. I just eat what I'm served."

"It's okay. Freedom takes time to accept," Emma said sadly. "Would you like me to order for you?"

"Yeah, thanks," I muttered.

Taylor practically dragged me from the house. I couldn't even believe I was doing this. I just prayed they were right and I didn't get in trouble for this. Aside from the escape, this was the most rebellious thing I'd ever done in my life.

She drove over to a big building with lots of cars in front of it and parked then told me to get out.

"What is this place?"

"A school."

We walked inside and she introduced me to the lady behind a big desk.

"This is Mirage. She's new in town. We'll only be here a few minutes. I need to see Shelby and Bella. Can we just go on back?"

"You know that's against the rules."

"It's important. You know I wouldn't be here if it weren't. I don't make a habit of disrupting class time. We'll only be a few minutes."

"Tell me this is official Force business."

Taylor grinned. "It is actually."

"Okay, just be quick about it."

"Thanks." She turned back to me. "Come on."

We walked down a hall to stand outside a door with a window.

"Before we go in, I want you to look, really look."

"It's a classroom where kids learn, right?"

She nodded. "It is."

Without knocking, she opened the door and stepped inside, giving a wave to the teacher at the front of the room.

"Alright, we have a few minutes. Pull out your practice books and write the sentence on the board three times for me. Remember to practice good penmanship."

Once the kids settled, she walked over to us.

"Hey T, what's up?"

"Sorry for the disruption. This is Mirage, Colin's mate."

"Oh, hey. I thought we were giving her time to settle in first."

"I know, but Callie called us all in for lunch."

She frowned. "Without me?"

"Sorry. It was a spur of the moment thing, and we couldn't exactly pull you out of class in the middle of the day."

She huffed. "I always miss the good stuff. But hi, I'm Shelby, Ben's mate."

"Hi."

"Can I speak with Bella for a minute?"

"Should I be concerned?"

"Not at all."

"Bella, come here please."

I watched a small child get up from her desk and walk over to Shelby.

"Yes, Mrs. Shelby?"

My eyes welled up with tears. It was her. The little girl from the auction that I'd had to sit there and watch as she was forced to perform inside the box before being sold off to the highest bidder.

"She's in school like a normal kid?"

Taylor smiled sadly. "Bella, this is Ms. Mirage. She's like you and just moved here."

"You're a witch too?" she whispered.

I nodded as tears spilled over my cheeks. I dropped down to my knees and hugged her. Taylor wasn't lying. She had rescued her and was letting her go to school and be a normal kid.

"Are you okay?" she whispered to me.

Her big innocent eyes looked up at me as I nodded.

"I'm great. Are you okay?"

She nodded and whispered again. "I really like it here."

We shared a look, and in a way, it was like seeing my childhood innocence as a very different story of life was written.

I was so overwhelmed by emotions that I knew I needed to get out of there.

"Are you okay?" Shelby asked.

I nodded. "Better than okay. Thank you."

I wasn't certain either of them understood just how much it meant to me to watch her walk back to her desk.

A little girl grabbed for her hand and whispered, "What was that about?"

Bella just shrugged and took her seat to write her sentences.

"It's so cool that you know Taylor," another kid said.

"Have you met Grant too? He's my favorite on the Force," someone else said.

"Yup. Grant's cool, I guess."

"What about Colin? He's my favorite," another kid said.

Bella giggled. "Yeah, he's funny."

It took me a minute to realize they were talking about my Colin like he was some kind of superhero. I considered that for a moment. For me he was a superhero, and definitely my favorite too.

"Thank you," Taylor said to Shelby. "Call me later."

"It was nice to meet you, Mirage."

I sniffed and wiped my eyes. "You too. Thank you for teaching her." I nearly choked on the words. I had been so very wrong about Taylor.

We didn't talk again until we were back in her car.

"You really did save her, didn't you?"

"Yeah. We try to get as many as possible without drawing attention to ourselves at the auctions. Walker and I are slowly establishing ourselves within the community. It hasn't been easy. Of course I want to rescue every single one of them, but how many more would we lose if we did that? I always look out for the kids. No one should grow up like that, Mirage. No one. You didn't deserve this, and you didn't do anything to warrant it. What they did to you was horrible, but I have to believe you are strong enough to overcome it. I know it's not easy right now and the rest of us take our freedom and independence for granted. I know it's going to take some time for you to adjust, but you aren't alone. Us Force mates stick together, and we protect each other. We're family. Bravo, Delta, it doesn't matter. We're all here for you and want to make this transition as easy as possible. But I can promise you that Bella will never live a life hidden away with rules that could mean the difference between life and death the way you did."

I started to sob and nodded. "Thank you."

She leaned over and hugged me while I cried.

"Now, how about that burger?"

"Okay."

We drove into town. The Crate turned out to be a bar. Taylor had to explain to me what that meant. I scrunched up my nose in disgust when she mentioned they sell alcohol. After tasting beer, I wasn't in a hurry to do it again.

"Hey, is everything okay?" Callie asked when she saw me.

"Better than okay," I admitted.

Taylor put her arm around me and squeezed.

"We decided that you need to start figuring out what you like and don't like, so I had Jesse make you a plain cheeseburger and a plate of all the toppings to try. And if we need another burger to keep sampling, just ask for it," Emma told me.

I took a deep breath and nodded. I could do this.

I looked at the plate before me. I'd had most of the things before.

"I don't like tomato or pickles," I confessed.

The ladies clapped and cheered me on.

"That's our girl. There's no need to eat what you don't like," Christine said.

"But I don't want to waste it either."

"Jesse, we need a trashcan," Taylor yelled across the room.

He rolled his eyes but appeased her.

"Okay Mirage. Now pick up the tomato and throw it in the trash," she instructed.

I shook my head. I couldn't possibly do that.

"Do it! Do it!" Emma started chanting.

Lachlan and a few of the guys were sitting at a nearby table and he got up to walk over to us.

"What are you up to?"

"Group therapy," Alaina told him.

"We're having an intervention," Taylor added. "Mirage, do it!"

I picked up the tomato and threw it in the trash as they erupted in cheers.

"How did that feel?" Taylor asked.

"Terrifying, and wonderful. My hand's shaking."

"Now the pickles," Christine insisted.

"Seriously, what are you doing?" Lachlan asked.

"Taking control of something in my life for the first time. I don't like pickles," I told him as I threw them in the trash. This time I joined them when they started cheering.

"Huh, good job, Mirage," he said before returning to his table.

I tried small bits of different topping combinations, throwing away the things I didn't like, and finally coming to the conclusion that I really only liked onions, ketchup, and mayonnaise on the burger.

"We have a winner," Emma announced, startling one of the triplets who was starting to dose off at the table.

I learned that the kids weren't hers, but actually Shelby's. Emma was just their nanny while Shelby worked.

"Poor thing. You should get the kids home," Vada said. "I can't believe my two actually slept through all this noise."

"Yeah, Kylie is being pleasant now, but she's going to be screaming to eat soon," Olivia confessed.

"Caleb too," Susan said with a sigh. "This was fun though. We should do it again soon."

"Definitely," Christine said. "It's nice to be able to join you guys during the day for once."

They got up and started saying goodbye to each other. I was surprised when I started getting included in that too.

Alaina hugged me first. "It was great to meet you."

"I am so proud of you, girl," Emma said holding out a fist as I flinched thinking she was going to punch me.

Taylor rolled her eyes and grabbed my hand, made a fist, and then bumped it against Emma's. "See you soon. Good job today. Just remember, baby steps. You're safe here, so break all those rules."

I nodded. I was starting to see what she was saying, though a part of me still worried that Colin would be upset about me leaving.

I had learned that only Callie and Christine were also Delta mates. The rest of them had mates on Bravo team. Once it was just the three of us, they showed me the park in the middle of town. It was beautiful and peaceful. I loved it there.

"What about Annie?" I asked them as we walked. "She's Tucker's mate, right?"

They both groaned.

"Annie takes some getting used to," Callie said.

"Yeah, and I'm still trying to get used to her."

They both cracked up.

"Tucker's a great guy so there has to be something in her that he sees. It's just sometimes hard for the rest of us to see it," Callie tried to explain.

"She's awful. He deserves so much better," Christine said.

Callie shot her a look. "We're trying to be supportive, remember?"

"I know. I'm sorry. I'm just struggling with how she behaved last night. I wanted to smack her. I can't believe he chose to mate her."

"What does that mean?"

"They aren't true mates. All the rest of us are."

"True mates? Colin said that about us."

"Oh yeah, you two are definitely true mates," Callie confirmed. "Anyone around you for more than two seconds can see that."

"You'll find a lot of true mates around here. The Westins have set that example for generations. I used to think it didn't matter. I just wanted a mate, but I was wrong. Finding Linc has changed my life. I feel whole for the first time."

"That's what I thought about Colin too. I still feel broken, but not in the same way as before," I confessed.

"You haven't completed your mating yet, have you?"

"What does that mean?"

"Has he marked you yet?"

I remembered what Colin had told me about that and how he would bite me and I'd bite him when the time came.

I shook my head.

"When you finally seal your bond, you may even find some of those cracks heal quickly too. I know they did for me."

"Are you ladies up for some shopping? I need to pick up a few things while I'm out," Callie said.

"Okay."

"I've never been shopping," I confessed.

"Well, let's fix that," she said.

We walked over to a larger standalone building still in town. They just walked in, the glass just moved to the sides for them and then closed behind them as I stood there gawking.

Chris came back out and grabbed my hands, pulling me inside with her.

"Automatic doors."

"Wow."

Inside was more food than I'd ever seen in my entire life.

"Woah! Is this for real?"

"Grocery store," Callie told me. "Restaurants like the Crate, Pino's, or Silver Bells will prepare food for you, whatever you like. But here at the grocery store you can buy foods to take home and make yourself."

I gulped hard. "Cook them myself?"

"Yup. Saves a lot of money and is easier than going out all the time."

"Money?" I whispered. "I don't have any money."

"You will. Westin Force should have already given you a stipend to get settled as well as a cell phone."

"A phone?"

"Yes. I'm surprised that hasn't already happened, especially with you still mating. Colin will go nuts if he can't get in touch with you. I'll talk to Michael about it tonight."

"And if you decide to officially give loyalty to Kyle and accept him as your Alpha, you'll have a pack payment each month too," Christine added.

"What about Colin?"

"He gets it too," she assured me. "That boy rarely spends money on anything but pizza. You aren't hurting for money."

"But that's his money," I argued.

She shrugged. "What's his is yours and what's yours is his. Once you seal your bond it'll be for life."

"Till death do us part, and if we're given enough time together that our bond fully seals, then even beyond this life," Callie said with a smile.

"You don't believe in divorce?" I asked.

"How do you know about divorce?" Christine asked.

I shrugged. "Movies."

She groaned. "Well, that's not the shifter way. We mate for life. Divorce is just a human thing."

I hadn't realized that.

As we walked up and down the aisles talking, I still couldn't stop gawking at just how much food was here. One of my Collectors had told me that food was scarce, and I should be grateful for every bit I got and never waste it, but here it was plentiful, and the others had made me throw food away. I really didn't know what to think anymore.

There was so much in this world that I still didn't understand. I couldn't even wrap my mind around some of the stuff they were saying. I was going to have my own money? I could buy my own food? It was insane to even think about. But I watched Callie do just that. It was amazing.

"Are you sure you don't want anything?"

"No, not yet."

I couldn't even begin to think of what I would buy when I had my own money or what I would do with it all.

"Hey, let's go to Sheila's. I bet you could use some new clothes and I have a special package I need to pick up," Christine said.

She winked at me, but I had no idea what she was talking about. Callie must have though as she started to laugh.

They explained that Sheila's was a small boutique that sold clothing.

"I ripped my clothes yesterday," I reminded them. "When I shifted."

"But that's not all the clothes you have, right?"

I shook my head. "I have this one and two others plus a swim suit."

"We're going to have to fix this. I have a few friends close to your size. I'll put out a request for things they aren't using, but you also need a few new things that are all yours. Come on, our treat," Chris said, holding out her hand and signaling I should walk ahead of them.

I took a deep breath. I could do this. I kept walking, but the door never opened.

"Ow," I whined when I ran right into it and fell backwards.

"Oh no. That's not an automatic door, just a regular one," Callie said.

I sighed. "How am I supposed to know the difference?"

Christine started laughing. "I don't really know, but if the door doesn't open for you on approach then it's a pretty big clue."

I groaned, but their laughing didn't bother me.

"I'm never going to understand this world."

"Yes, you will. You're doing great," Callie assured me with a little laugh. "Sorry, but you should have seen the look of shock on your face."

She held out a hand and pulled me back to my feet.

This time, Chris opened the door and held it open for me.

Inside there were stacks and stacks of clothing, piles of things everywhere.

"This is insane."

"This is a very small store. Someday, we'll take you into town and show you a big department store. It'll blow your mind," Callie said.

*This already is,* I thought but didn't say.

"Hello ladies. What can I do for you?"

"Sheila, this is Mirage, Colin's mate."

"Colin's? I hadn't heard. Wow, all the handsome ones seem to be falling hard lately. Welcome to San Marco, Mirage. Now, what can I do for you?"

"She arrived with only the clothes on her back. She's picked up a few things since, but not much, and one of her outfits ripped yesterday shifting," Callie explained.

"Oh you poor thing. I have a bag of clothes in the back that I was just about to donate to the clothing bank. Let me grab it."

She left and returned with two large trash bags full of clothes.

"Start here and feel free to take anything you'd like. She'll need a few new things too, so I'll start pulling a few things for that while you look."

They made me try on tons of clothes and helped me pick out a few new outfits and a bag full of the stuff she said I could just take.

"Oh, also, did my package come in?" Christine asked just as we were about to leave.

"Yes, it did. Want to come back and take a look around?" Sheila offered.

"Absolutely."

"It's um, sex toys. Do you want to go see?" Callie asked.

"Sure," I said. I had no idea what she was even talking about, but Christine seemed pretty excited about it.

The path to get there had no windows and was already giving me bad vibes and reminders of some horrible places I'd been forced to endure.

*I am strong.*
*I am beautiful.*
*I am powerful.*
*I am a fighter.*
*I will survive.*
*I can do this,* I told myself.

I should have turned back, but I held my head high and continued right up until I walked into the room and immediately saw various torture devices hanging on the far wall. There was a whip and leather bindings.

Memories of screams surfaced in my head as I closed my eyes and covered my ears feeling paralyzed.

Callie noticed my reaction immediately and got me out of there as quickly as possible. Outside, I gulped in fresh air and sat down on the curb as I pulled my knees up to my chest and rocked back and forth mumbling to myself.

"I am strong.

I am beautiful.

I am powerful.

I am a fighter.

I will survive."

"That's a beautiful mantra, Mirage," Callie said. "I'm sorry. We weren't thinking about possible triggers in there for you. Did they hurt you?"

There was no judgement in her eyes when I looked up.

"Not me, at least not in that way. But I witnessed plenty, especially in my earlier collections. They'd chain them to the walls and beat them while having sex. I swore I'd never have sex or let someone touch me like that. Anytime I felt threatened like that, I would hide behind my powers. Collectors don't like you using your powers against them. It got me kicked out of more than one. I was traded more than most."

"I'm glad. Wait, did you say no sex? Does Colin know this about you yet? It sounded like you were headed in that direction when we all discreetly bailed last night."

I blushed furiously. "I didn't know that's what I was doing, the first time, at least. It was an accident."

She burst out laughing. "This I have to hear. How do you accidentally have sex?"

I shrugged and grinned. "I was just doing what felt natural. I didn't know that's what it was." I groaned. "This is so embarrassing.

I can't believe I just told you that. Obviously, it wasn't like I was expecting sex to be."

"Ah, so you liked it, then."

My cheeks felt like they were on fire.

"It's okay. There's nothing to be embarrassed about, and you're right, sex is the most natural thing in the world, designed to make us feel really good, as long as it's with a person you trust and care about. Your true mate is the best you'll ever have too. Trust me, that is coming from someone who didn't wait and wish I had."

I nodded, happy to realize I actually knew what she meant. Sometimes they would say stuff that was completely over my head, and I just had to guess at what they meant.

"And you're right. You are strong. You are beautiful. You are powerful. You are a fighter, and you will not only survive here, but thrive, because you are a survivor. And you're smart too. You should add that one to your mantra next time."

I leaned my head on her shoulder and whispered. "I hope you're right."

Christine came running out with a package in hand.

"Is she okay?"

"I'm fine," I said, answering for myself. I stared up at the package in her hand. "You bought something?"

"Yeah. I've been waiting for it to come in. Wanna see?"

I looked to Callie for help.

"How hardcore are we talking here?"

"What? No. Oh God! Is that what happened?" She growled and sat next to me, pulling me from Callie and holding me.

"A little too tight," I protested.

Colin had warned me that wolves were very touch driven. I'd been hugged more today than the rest of my life combined.

"It's nothing like that. Just a pretty, new lingerie set."

She looked around and then opened the box and showed us a lacy dark-purple thing.

"That's not going to cover much," I warned her.

"And that's the point. Don't worry, it's for Lincoln's eyes only."

"Oh," I said. "Would Colin like something like that?"

"Definitely," they both said.

"I don't think I can handle going back in there. Not yet."

"It's okay. It's not going anywhere. If you want something I'm happy to run in and pick it out for you. She already has your measurements."

*Be courageous*, I told myself. "Okay," I told her.

"Okay?" Callie asked. "Are you sure?"

"As long as I don't have to go back into that room. It's just pretty underwear, right?"

"Basically," Christine agreed.

"And Colin would like it?"

"Most definitely."

"It'll most certainly lead to other things," Callie tried to discreetly tell me.

"Oh, I don't mind that part at all. I like it," I assured her. She grinned.

"I didn't know!" I blurted out again.

"What's going on?" Chris asked.

"Don't worry about it. Just go pick her out something sexy, not one that you need an engineering degree to figure out how to wear."

Chris laughed but ran off to pick something out for me. She was back in record time as she passed me the box.

"I went with blue. It'll really accentuate your eyes."

I dared a peek into the box.

"Oh, yeah, that's really pretty." It was nearly as scandalous as the sheer all-lace piece she had bought. This one was a mix of lace and satin. I was excited to get home and try it on. "Thanks."

"Anytime. I'm kind of addicted to the place, so anytime you want something, just let me know."

Callie got a call and had to leave us. I was sad to see her go, but we were already making plans to get together again soon.

Christine drove me home, but also bailed soon after claiming she wanted to be home waiting to surprise Linc when he got there.

I was completely alone in the house once more, but things had changed for me throughout the day. Feeling a newfound sense of confidence, I opened the oven and tossed the pizzas inside. And then I went to the refrigerator and opened the door. I was looking for anything that might go with pizza, but there was a stench of rotten food in there, so I closed it quickly and abandoned the thought. Pizza would have to do, again.

Taking a deep breath, I started to wander around and really look around the house. I had never been the curious type or a troublemaker. For the most part, I was a rule follower. The only times I rebelled against them were when I felt like my life was in danger.

"This isn't breaking any rules. He said I could look around the house," I told myself aloud, justifying my decision to snoop.

With each step I took up the stairs, I felt stronger and more in control of my own life than ever before. He'd offered me freedom and I was ready to take it.

\*\*\*\*\*

*One week later.*

"I can't believe we have to say goodbye," I cried, giving Boris a hug.

Over the last week I'd been busy settling into my new life in Westin Pack. After spending the day with the girls, I'd felt empowered to help. I'd survived for a reason, and there were still so many out there that were still stuck in captivity.

I was never going to be a superhero like Colin, going around the world rescuing people the way he'd rescued me and my friends, but I had a lot more information about many collections. Things I hadn't even realized.

The one female on the Force that I hadn't met during what I now called my first day of freedom was Marie. She was a witch too. Her power was a little scary. She could look into a person's eyes and see right into their soul—every memory, past, present, and even future if you consider plans and dreams.

We hit it off pretty quickly, and she convinced me to let her try and pull information regarding locations and details of the various collections I'd been in. She was able to get addresses, general locations, inside layouts, and all sorts of information from me, stuff I never would have thought about or remembered but was apparently still stored up in my brain somewhere.

We were having pretty regular sessions now as she continued looking for anything that could help the teams take these collections down. They were already busy making plans for their next mission, and I was so proud to have played even a small part in it.

Some of the others had agreed to sessions with Marie too.

"You keep fighting the good fight, Mirage," Boris said as he hugged me one final time.

I hated to see him go but we were all thrilled that his family had been located and he was going home. He even got to video chat with them where he learned he had twin boys that were now eight. He hadn't even known his mate was pregnant when he was captured. She told him they were what got her through every day in his absence. He couldn't wait to reunite with them.

I tried to imagine what it would be like to be separated from Colin like that, but it just gave me panic attacks to even think about it.

"You hug those boys from us too. I'm so happy for you, but I'm going to miss you like crazy," I told him.

"I have my new phone and promise to keep in touch. You have my number. Call anytime."

"I will," I promised as I stood back and let him say goodbye to the others.

Atlas walked over and wrapped an arm around my shoulders as I leaned into him.

"Everything's changed."

"That's not a bad thing."

"I know. I've never been happier, but our little collection wasn't so bad most of the time. I'm going to miss him."

"They don't know how to tell you, but the girls are leaving too. They'll be heading out in a few days."

"What? All of them?"

"Not Ramona. She's staying, as are me and Ned."

My heart hurt losing my family, even knowing I already had another that I loved.

"This is really happening?"

"Yup. Are you okay?"

"Yeah. As long as they are free and happy, I'm happy for them."

"I tried to tell them you would be. If the rest of you need to go and find your own path, I will understand, too. My life is here now."

"My clan was never comfortable with my powers. I mean, bears pride themselves on strength. It's glorified, but apparently not when you're this strong."

"I'm so sorry."

"Don't be. It's their loss."

"I've talked to Baine a great deal about it, and he raves about this place. I'm going to stick around and give it a chance."

"I'm glad. I'm not ready to lose you."

"And what about me?" Ned asked. "I'm staying too."

"Have you been adopted by Nonna yet?"

"Hell no! The stories of that woman scare the shit out of me. I'm going to steer clear of her for as long as possible."

I laughed. I'd met Nonna and I strongly suspected she'd eat Ned alive.

"Okay, well, I need to run by the store and pick up a few things, but I'll catch up with you guys later."

"Look at you. I'm so proud of you. Are you really going to the store all by yourself?"

"I am. I think I'm ready. I'm attempting to make dinner for Colin and me tonight."

Ned pursed his lips and tried not to laugh.

"It's not funny, Ned. How was I supposed to know you had to turn the oven on to heat up pizza?"

My first day of freedom hadn't exactly gone all that smoothly. I'd been so proud of myself when Colin came home on my first day of freedom. I'd tossed the remainder of the pizza into the oven just like he told me, but I didn't know it had to be turned on and heated up first. So I pulled out still cold pizza to serve to him, but God love him, he ate every bite without complaint.

Everyone else seemed to get a good laugh from it though when I'd mistakenly confessed it to Atlas.

I glared at him now. "I told you that in confidence."

"It was just too good to keep to myself."

"Whatever. I'll see you guys tomorrow."

"Make sure the door opens this time," Ned yelled at my retreating back.

I whipped around and glared at Atlas. "Do you just blab everything to him now?"

"My best friend has been a little busy. I had to find someone to confide in."

"You suck."

"You love me."

"Good thing for you."

I left them, shaking my head. I'd been practicing driving a car, but I wasn't completely comfortable with it yet. Taylor had agreed to drive me to the store and then home.

"Hey."

"Are you ready for this?"

"Yes," I told her honestly. "Or as ready as I'm going to be."

"Do you want me to go in with you?"

"Nope. I need to do this on my own."

"Okay. I'll be in the store if you change your mind but even if we cross paths, I'll pretend I have no clue who you are."

"Sounds great."

We chatted on the drive into town. I was nervous but more excited. I'd been taking baby steps towards this all week. I had my list, and I knew I could do this.

"Good luck," Taylor said as I got out of the car.

I walked right up to the door but hesitated for a fraction of a second to ensure it opened before walking through. I breathed a sigh of relief once inside.

The lady at the cash register waved at me and gave me a thumbs up when she saw no one was with me.

Everyone in Westin Pack had been amazing, rallying behind me on my quest for independence. I didn't want to let them down, but I also didn't think I would ever have true independence when I needed Colin as desperately as I did.

Sex every night, most mornings, and during occasional lunch breaks had become like an addiction to me and my favorite parts of each day. I was crazy about my mate and ready to claim him, even though we hadn't talked about it anymore and I hadn't told him my feelings either.

He was mine and I'd kill anyone who got in the way of that.

Taking out my list, I started in the produce aisle. I was making a basic Caesar salad and spaghetti for dinner with toasted garlic bread. I was cheating and picking up a cheesecake for dessert though. Dumping a bag of lettuce and mixing in the toppings from the bag was something I could handle. I was a little nervous about the noodles, but I was confident I could handle heating up a jar of sauce. The problem came when Taylor noted the lack of meat and suggested I brown some hamburger, sausage, or both to the sauce.

Grabbing the bag of salad, I moved to the back of the store to the butcher.

"Hi Samson."

"Well, hello, Mirage." He looked around to see who was with me.

"I'm shopping solo today," I told him proudly.

"Fantastic. How can I help?"

"I'm attempting to cook dinner tonight. I'm doing spaghetti and need a meat to add to the sauce."

"Okay. Hamburger or sausage?"

I shrugged. "I don't really know the difference."

"Okay, let's talk options. Ground meat goes well in sauce, but meatballs or sausage links could be easier for a first timer."

"I like easy."

"Okay, meatballs you just need to toss in the oven."

I groaned. "The last time someone told me that, they failed to mention I had to turn the oven on first and we ate cold pizza. I haven't tried cooking again since. I don't want a repeat of that."

He chuckled but then he froze. He was distracted by something behind the counter.

"Hi Miss Mirage," a sweet voice said, and I turned around to see Bella.

"Hi sweetie. How are you?"

"Good. I lost another tooth." She opened her mouth and showed me.

"That's great. I can already see the new one coming in."

"You can?" she asked excitedly.

"Yup."

There was a mirror up towards the ceiling to allow people to see around the corner safely. Something caught my attention, and I looked up, then did a double take and gasped.

"Shit!"

"Mirage," Samson whispered in a very low octave. "Behind the counter, now."

My heart was pumping hard, and I was nearly paralyzed in fear until Bella's little hand took mine.

"Are you okay?"

"Now," Samson said.

I shook off the fear and grabbed Bella, cupping my hand over her mouth. Her eyes widened and I could smell her fear, but there was no time to explain. I had to protect her.

Picking her up, I carried her behind the counter with Samson and sank to the floor, curled up as tightly as possible.

I held my finger to my lips and Bella nodded so I removed my hand.

"Can I help you?" Samson asked.

"Maybe. Have you seen this woman?"

That voice sent chills down my spine as I started shaking all over.

Bella gripped my arm tighter as if she sensed my fear too. Big tears welled up in her eyes.

Taylor was here. He could recognize her, too. I had to warn her.

I dared a quick glimpse through the meat counter. He was right there, and Taylor was just rounding the corner.

"Nope, can't say I have," Samson finally replied.

"How about any of these," he asked, handing a stack of photos to Samson.

I was trapped and didn't know how to get Taylor's attention. My phone fell out of my pocket and clattered to the floor.

"What was that?" the Collector asked.

"Nothing important. Just kicked something." Samson looked down and shot me a look to knock it off.

My phone!

I picked it up and quickly texted Taylor.

ME: Run and hide. He's here. He'll recognize you.

TAYLOR: I don't care. Where are you?

ME: Samson

TAYLOR: Stay put. Help is on the way.

"Bella?" I heard a woman call out. "Samson, have you seen Bella?"

"I believe she's with Grant," he said.

I grabbed Bella's arm and shook my head. She started crying as I held her close to me.

ME: I have Bella

TAYLOR: Thanks. I'll intercept her mom.

"Bella?" the woman walked away calling again.

"Kids," Samson said. "Always wandering off."

"She's over here," a male sounding voice said.

I had no doubt Taylor was intercepting the issue.

Bella scooted closer to me and knocked something over.

"What was that?" the Collector asked again.

"Nothing you need to worry about. I haven't seen any of these people."

Still, he didn't move on.

"I don't believe you."

"Believe what you want, man."

"They have to be here. I've looked everywhere else. They came here first. Why? What's here?"

"We're just a small town in the mountains. If they were here, I don't know about it, but then people around here like their privacy. They don't take too kindly to people snooping around here either."

"Is that a warning, old man?"

"Take it how you'd like."

"They're here. You're hiding them. I know it. Come out, my pets."

I desperately looked around for an exit, but I was trapped.

"I know they're here and I can prove it," he yelled out.

Suddenly my entire body was wracked with shockwaves of pain. I closed my eyes and held my breath. I couldn't risk alerting him to my presence. I couldn't react to this. I cloaked Bella and I wondered why I hadn't thought to do that sooner.

*I am strong.*

*I am beautiful.*

*I am powerful.*

*I am a fighter.*

*I will survive.*

*I can do this.*

Gritting my teeth, I refused to cry out from the pain as I laid on the floor withering in pain.

"Excuse me, can I help you with something?"

The pain eased off some.

"I want to report a kidnapping."

"Who exactly was kidnapped?"

"My p…," he cleared his throat. "My charges. It would appear they've run away, and I'm greatly concerned for their safety."

"Okay, well you can come down to the station and we'll file a report."

I heard a growl and felt Colin's presence nearby. He was here, and he was going to make everything better. Relief took away the last of the pain, until I realized he was in his fur. I had to do something and quickly.

# Colin

## Chapter 25

I was in the gym with the team working out when an alarm went off on our phones. I grabbed mine to check what was going on.

ALERT: Grocery store.

"I can go check it out," I volunteered. "I'm due at the station for a perimeter run today with the new volunteers anyway."

"Thanks. That would be great. It's probably nothing or one of the kids trying to steal a bag of chips or something," Michael teased.

ALERT: Code Red.

ALERT: Mirage.

My stomach churned and I wanted to throw up.

Michael was already calling it in while signaling the full team to move out.

"This is Delta one confirming a code red."

I was close enough to hear his conversation. Sometimes wolf hearing came in handy.

"Code red confirmed. There's a man walking around with pictures asking if anyone's seen them. Mirage was one of them."

"Okay. Colin, stay calm and find your mate."

I started to leave, and then froze at the next words that came through the phone.

"She's here in the store."

"Shit! We're on our way."

He led the way out at a full run with the team falling in place behind him.

Walker's phone rang and he ignored it, but when it immediately rang again, he answered. "T, this isn't a good time right now."

"Luther is here," I heard her tell him.

"Do you have eyes on Mirage?"

"Sort of. She texted me. I think Samson is hiding her behind the meat counter but Luther's there questioning him, and he has the button pressed."

"What button?" Walker asked.

I growled.

Grabbing my phone, I called Lane.

"Hey, are you calling to cancel on me today?"

"There's a code red at the grocery store. The Collector is there flashing pictures around asking questions. Mirage is there and trapped. We're en route, but you're closer. Please. My mate is in danger."

"Callie, Jenkins, code red at the grocery store. Let's go. It's Mirage. Delta is on the way."

Satisfied they would do what they could to protect her, I shifted and took off as fast as I could the second I stepped outside the Lodge. All I could see was red. My mate was in trouble.

In record time I was at the grocery store and running in my fur. My team had shifted too and were right behind me.

No one in the store batted an eye our way.

As I was running for the meat counter, Lane was already there talking to him and escorting him out.

Michael took the lead and snapped at me to get behind him. Still, I cut loose with a low and menacing growl that startled the guy.

Suddenly there was another growl coming from behind him. I relaxed a little when I saw my mate but was furious that she had just exposed herself to him. She wasn't alone though. Half a dozen other wolves rounded the corner surrounding him.

He screamed and tried to jump into Lane's arms.

"You have to protect me. It's your job. Don't let them hurt me!" he screeched.

Without even cracking a smile, Lane looked at him like he was crazy.

"Sir, are you feeling okay?"

"What? Are you crazy? They're everywhere?"

"Who?"

I had to give him credit, Lane kept his cool and delivered a flawless performance that would have given Birdie a run for her money.

"The wolves!"

He actually looked around without any recognition whatsoever except a quick wink my way letting me know he had this under control.

"Sir, there are no wolves here. Is there someone I can call for you?" he asked with a straight face.

"Are you insane? Or just blind?" the Collector was yelling as Lane escorted him out.

Samson rounded the corner still in his skin.

"You. Yes, you. You see them too, don't you?"

He looked around and furrowed his brow.

"See what?"

"The wolves. They're everywhere! Tell them."

"I don't see any wolves."

"Are you crazy? There's one right there next to you."

Samson turned to the rack of food and picked up a pack of gummies with wolf pups on it and showed him.

"The kids sure do love these things, but I promise, they're harmless wolves."

"Not those wolves! Those," he said, pointing around to all of us as more and more wolves joined us. "Oh no. They're multiplying!"

I kept my eyes on him the entire time but suspected every person in the store had shifted. Even the cashiers were in their fur on their hind legs, only contributing to the guy's hysteria.

"It's a conspiracy. You're all in on it. You're witches. All of you. Wolf witches. I'm going to expose you to the world. Everyone will come here hunting you. The whole world will know I'm not crazy!"

Callie was following her boss's lead as she made a call.

"Yes, we have a situation here in San Marco. Requesting an ambulance with restraints. This guy is high as a kite on something or just having a nervous breakdown. He's saying he's seeing wolves everywhere… Of course, I'm aware of the folklore of the area, but this one's taking that to a whole new level claiming they're shopping at the grocery store… Great. He'll be cooling off in a cell until you get up here… Sure, we can do that. I'll call him next. Thanks."

When she hung up, she made another call. "Micah, it's Callie. We have a situation. Willis General is sending an ambulance up to retrieve an unruly tourist claiming to see wolves throughout the grocery store and harassing the workers there. They've requested to have you sedate him heavy enough for them to get up the mountain and safely back down with him… Great. Meet us at the station."

Lane already had him out of the store and was shoving him into the back of his cruiser.

I ran back to Mirage as soon as they pulled away and drove out of sight. I rubbed up against her, checking her all over to ensure she wasn't hurt. She shifted back to her skin, crying as she threw her arms around my neck and buried her head in my fur.

I forced myself to shift back so I could hold her. Others started shifting back to their skin too. They were watching us.

"Mess with one wolf, face the pack," Samson said.

Cheers and howls sounded off throughout the room.

"Thank you," I told him, standing up to shake his hand.

"Bella," Mirage said as she turned and ran to the back of the store.

I ran after her. No way was she leaving my sight anytime soon. My wolf was still on edge and would continue to be until I knew for damn sure that asshole was out of our territory.

She dropped down behind the counter and little arms wrapped around her neck.

"It's over. He's gone."

Taylor ran over to us. "Oh, thank God."

The woman with her took the child from Mirage.

"This is Lisa. She's fostering Bella until we can find a family to adopt her."

"Thank you for watching after her. I hope she wasn't any trouble. She ran off, and I couldn't find her anywhere, and then the craziness began." She looked down at the girl and scolded her. "You can't run off like that, Bella."

"It wasn't her fault. I took her. The man that was here was looking for me, but he had seen Bella before too." Mirage didn't go into any more detail than that, probably knowing that others were listening in.

Instead, she turned around and grabbed a piece of paper and wrote down her phone number.

"Oh, well that certainly changes things," Lisa said.

She ignored her and bent over to Bella's level. "This is my cell number. If there is ever anything you need, call me. If you just get scared and need someone to talk to, call me. Okay?"

The little girl nodded and then hugged her. "Thanks Miss Mirage." Then she looked up at me. "Are you Colin?"

"I am."

"You're my best friend's favorite. Whenever we play Westin Force, she always wants to be you."

Mirage beamed up at me and stood back up. "You have a fan club."

I shrugged. "That's cool as long as you're still my number one fan."

Before she could protest, I kissed her.

"Always."

"Wait, you're Mirage's mate?"

"I am," I proudly told Bella.

"Well now you're my favorite as well. I can't wait to tell Emmalyn tomorrow."

"Come on, Bella. We need to get home. Bye, and thanks again."

I waved at them both. And then noticed Sheila running around with clothes and blankets to pass out. I signaled her over to us and accepted clothes for the both of us.

"Are you okay, Mirage?" she asked.

"No, but I will be. This guy will see to it."

Pride swelled within my chest at her confidence in me. I hadn't let her down. I was there, exactly where I needed to be, and she was safe. That was all that mattered.

"Get dressed. I still have work to do, and I'm not about to let you out of my sight, maybe not ever after that."

"I'm okay with that," she confessed, pressing a kiss to my lips before doing as I asked.

Only when she was dressed did my team approach us.

"She okay?" Michael asked.

"Not a scratch on her. She's too smart for that."

She beamed up at me and love shone through her eyes, hitting me hard right in the chest.

I was in love with my mate.

That revelation didn't scare me in the least. I already knew I wanted to claim her and spend the rest of my life with her. There was still so much more to learn about my mate, but we had a lifetime ahead of us for that.

"What?" she asked.

I shook my head. "I'll tell you later."

"We're going to head over to the station. Silas is meeting me there. We're going to let him keep his crazy but change some of his past memories including why he ever came here. I'm confident we can keep your mate safe here, despite today's breach."

"Short of putting up a blockade, there's no way to stop a breach that just drives up the mountain and right into town," I reminded him.

"Maybe. We'll start brainstorming new efforts. The emergency system worked well though."

"It did. Don't worry. I'm okay."

"Okay. Still, add two more weeks with Lachie for me?"

I groaned. "Fine."

"Really? No complaints?" he asked skeptically.

"Nope. After this I'm sure I have plenty to rant about."

He laughed as Lachlan groaned.

"Good luck with that, man," Tucker teased him.

Since finding Mirage, I'd really been opening up a lot more about my feelings and the things that were bothering me. Lachlan was probably sick of hearing me talk this past week, but he'd get over it.

"Can we join you at the station?" I asked.

"No. It's not worth the risk having her there, and I'm not dumb enough to ask you to leave her right now. So take your mate home, take the rest of the day off, and enjoy your weekend. We'll keep you updated, but this is the time when you need to trust your team to have your back."

"Aside from this girl, there's no others I trust more."

He hugged me, one by one the others did too.

"Ready?"

"Mirage," Samson called out. "Do you still want those meatballs?"

She laughed. "Not today. I think we're just going to order pizza. That's probably more my cooking skill-level anyway."

"Samson, thanks for taking care of my mate."

If word hadn't already sufficiently spread through the Pack regarding my mating status, it would now. I needed to claim her. This was a first step towards that.

"Let's go home," I said.

"Yes, please."

Taking Michael's advice, I took my mate straight back to the house.

"So what were you doing in the grocery store anyway?"

She blushed. "I wanted to surprise you and cook dinner."

I smiled while trying really hard not to laugh as I recalled the last time she attempted to surprise me with dinner and didn't know she had to turn the oven on to heat up the leftover pizza.

"Don't laugh," she said, elbowing me in the ribcage.

"I'm not," I lied. "What were you going to cook?"

"Salad, spaghetti, and garlic bread."

"That's one of my favorites."

"I know. You told me. I was going to surprise you."

"How about we pick a night and make it together instead? I'm a decent cook and can teach you."

"Really?"

"Of course."

She leaned over and kissed me as I tried to keep one eye on the road and pull into the driveway. Once parked safely, I pulled her into my lap and kissed her harder.

"Take me to bed, Colin."

I opened the door and pulled her out with me as she wrapped her legs around my waist, and I ran us all the way into the house.

Kicking the front door shut, I braced her up against it and made quick work of removing her shirt.

She moaned and fisted her hands in my hair as I found her breast with my mouth and feasted there.

Sex with Mirage had gotten hot quickly. She was a fast learner, and I was more than happy to teach her exactly what I needed and was a studious learner of what she liked most.

"Yes!" she cried out. "But I need you inside me right now."

I was still feeling very territorial over her and happy to oblige. I stopped and slid her back down to the floor long enough to claw each other's clothes off.

"Bedroom?" I asked.

"Yes."

We didn't always do it in the bedroom anymore. In fact, we'd probably christened every inch of the house over the last week. There was no place in this house that I could look at and not see her there.

She jumped up on the bed, and I just stood there staring at her.

"I love you so much," I blurted out.

"Good, so claim me. I'm already yours and I'm not going anywhere. You told me once that it was my life, my choice. Well I'm telling you my choice is made. You are my mate, my sanctuary, my protector, and the only man I want waking up next to me every day for the rest of my life."

"Really?"

She nodded. "Oh, and I love you, too. So claim me already."

I grinned. She didn't have to tell me twice.

Growling, I sunk my teeth into her neck, marking her as mine forever, and waited to feel the pinch of her canines in return.

Peace and love filled me. This was it for me, my destiny, and the reason I didn't die that day Linc took a bullet for me. I'd never thought of it quite like that before, but now I was going to have to thank that sonofabitch and not out of guilt this time.

But first, I needed my mate in every way possible. This was the start of a whole new life for me, for both of us. and we were going to make the most of it every single day starting right now.

# Mirage

## Epilogue

*One Month Anniversary*

It was amazing how much my life has changed in just one month. I supposed when I was first taken and sold off to my very first Collector that life changed just as quickly with me, but I had mostly blacked out that time in my life.

For twenty years life was pretty predictable. I had rules to follow and a very sheltered life. It was easy and mostly unchanging right up until Colin walked into it and threw out the rulebook.

Sometimes I still wondered if I was really cut out for this world. I didn't always understand things and I made a lot of mistakes, but Colin just reminded me that was all part of the learning process.

Today I was going to attempt to surprise him once more. Together we'd cooked lots of meals and I was even getting pretty decent in the kitchen, but I still hadn't tried it solo yet. The last time hadn't exactly gone as planned.

We had a busy day planned so I needed to move quickly while he was at work this morning. My first stop was the grocery store.

I quickly ran to grab a bag of Caesar salad before heading back to see Samson.

"Mirage, what can I do for you today?"

"I'm going to need those meatballs."

He winked at me. "You've got it. Do you remember how to make them?"

"I do and I'm ready this time."

"See, that's why you're my favorite."

"Hey now, I thought I was your favorite," a woman said from behind me.

I whipped around to find Kelsey Westin standing behind me.

"Oh, hi Kelsey."

"Hello. Are you ready for today?"

"Yes," I said without hesitation.

"I don't know if you have any plans for tonight, but Kyle will insist you guys stay for dinner tonight. So, if you have any requests, let me know."

My face fell. "Do we have to?"

Samson chuckled. "Kiddo, when the Pack Mother and Alpha invite you to dinner, you just say yes."

I sighed. "Okay."

"Is it really that bad?" she asked with a chuckle.

"It's fine, it's just that it's our anniversary. One month since Colin and I met, and I really wanted to cook him a special meal all by myself. I haven't done that yet. But I suppose it will have to wait."

"Well not after you put it like that." She laughed. "Go ahead and make your special meal. I'll break the news to Kyle ahead of time but only if you promise we can have you both over for dinner soon."

"Any other night. This one's just kind of special."

"That's really sweet. I hope it works out for you."

"Me too. I'm a little nervous about it."

"About the meal or today?"

"Just the meal. Colin wanted to make a big deal about today. If it were up to me, I would just bow before you now and get it over with."

She laughed again. "Pretty sure Kyle wants to be there too."

I rolled my eyes. "Fine but let me go so I can get everything prepped before he gets home. I'll see you this afternoon."

"Don't forget your meatballs."

"Thanks Samson," I said as I grabbed them and quickly found the remainder of things I needed.

I drove myself home in my brand new car that Colin had surprised me with. Just another major change in my life.

The best thing I'd ever done was mate that man. He went out of his way to make me feel special and appreciated. I just wanted to do the same for him.

Once home I got to work quickly. This time I turned the oven on and let it heat up before putting the meatballs in. I'd certainly learned my lesson on that one. Next, I put a pot of water on to boil while I tossed the salad together and put it in a container to keep in the fridge.

Knowing I was short on time I ran to the bedroom and jumped into the shower to wash up before returning to put the meatballs in and the pasta on.

I set a timer for the pasta as I'd had a few mishaps with overcooking it in the past. Mostly because Colin was a huge distraction in the kitchen. Without him here, it should come out perfect.

I looked at the counter next to the stove and blushed before running down the hall and getting dressed before the buzzer went off.

It worked and I had perfectly cooked pasta.

I didn't bother heating the sauce, I just transferred the noodles into a casserole dish and then dumped the sauce in along with the meatballs when they were finished. Then I topped it all with cheese and covered it in aluminum foil to store in the fridge.

Dinner was basically ready. It just needed to be tossed into the oven, a concept I actually understood and could now execute.

Feeling proud and accomplished, I washed up the dishes and ensured the stove top and oven were turned off before I finished getting ready.

I was almost done when Colin came in to shower. It was tempting to join him, but he seemed anxious.

"We're going to be late."

"No, we're not," I assured him. "Just take a quick shower."

I picked up my phone when it dinged a few minutes later.

TAYLOR: Turn the news on NOW. Channel 12.

It took me a minute to find the remote and the right channel. Colin was just stepping out of the shower.

"Breaking news. Agriculture tycoon Luther Carrington IV declared mentally unstable today. All assets have been frozen as his nephew assumes control of Carrington Enterprise. 'My uncle is receiving the best care possible. At this time the family has no further comment,' says Arthur Carrington."

In the background there was a picture of Luther in a strait jacket yelling, "The wolves are coming. You have to listen to me. You need to believe. Beware of the wolves."

"Those at channel 12 wish him the best of luck in his recovery. Next up…"

"Looks like he's going to be put away for quite some time, sweetheart."

"Thank everything. That may be the best news yet."

"Are you ready?" he asked.

I turned to look at him. "Wow. You look handsome."

He beamed and leaned over to kiss me.

I shooed him away. "You're going to mess up my makeup."

"You always look gorgeous. You don't need makeup."

I just smiled back at him. I had already learned there was no point in arguing with him. He walked me out to the car and opened the door for me, before running around to his side and hopping into the driver's seat.

He held my hand while he drove. Somehow that simple motion made me feel special.

"I might have sort of invited a few people to join us today."

"Okay."

He seemed nervous, but I didn't know why. I wasn't going to change my mind.

There were a lot of cars in front of the Alpha house when we pulled up.

"How many's a few?" I asked.

He gave me a sheepish look. "It's not my fault. Everyone loves you and wants to be here to celebrate with you."

"It's not that big of a deal."

"It is to me, and a lot of other people."

"You said a few."

"Semantics."

I groaned but waited for him to get out and come around to open the door for me.

"We said we were keeping this lowkey."

"I know, I know. I'm sorry."

The door to the Alpha House flew open before we even reached it.

"Hi. I don't believe we've had a chance to meet yet. I'm Mary Westin. Please come in."

"Hi Mary."

Colin leaned down and kissed her cheek.

"Come on in, everyone's inside waiting."

She surprised me by hugging me next. It shouldn't have been a surprise. Everyone seemed to hug everyone in Westin Pack.

"I know we haven't met yet, but it already feels like you're Pack."

"Thanks," I told her unsure how else to respond.

Inside was everyone I cared most about. All of Delta and their mates. Most of Bravo team and their mates had come as well. And in the middle of it all stood Atlas, Ned, and Ramona.

"Guys, you all didn't need to be here."

"Of course we did," Callie said. "This is a big moment for you and as your family, we want to be here for you."

"Okay, but let's not make a huge deal of it, okay?"

"Why don't we get this over with quickly. Mom made a ton of food and we can hang out and talk afterwards," Kyle suggested.

"Sorry," Kelsey mouthed.

I smiled and shrugged. As I looked around, I realized this was exactly what I wanted for today.

"Alpha, Pack Mother, I would like to request acceptance of my allegiance to you both and to Westin Pack."

The room went quiet.

They looked at each other and smiled. "We accept."

I dropped to my knees in submission and bared my neck to them.

"Rise," Kyle said.

Ned started to snicker. "Sorry. That just seemed so regal and formal."

"It is formal," Colin explained.

"Rise," Ned mimicked Kyle.

Ramona smacked him. "Are you trying to get us kicked out or killed?"

"I'm sorry. Carry on," he said, bowing to them.

Kyle groaned and shook his head. "I'm starting to regret letting that one stay."

"Hey," Ned protested, making us all laugh.

Kelsey hugged me. "Welcome to the Pack, Mirage."

"Welcome home," Kyle said, making my eyes water.

"Thank you both."

Colin wrapped his arms around me and lifted me into the air. Then kissed me in front of everyone as they clapped and cheered.

"See that wasn't so bad."

"It was like five seconds. I'm just saying we didn't need all this fanfare for that."

"But we all wanted to be here," Callie insisted.

"Speak for yourself," I heard Annie mutter under her breath.

"Thank you, everyone. Really. You've all been so supportive and understanding through this last month and I can't thank you enough for everything."

"Refreshments are out. Please help yourself," Mary announced as she dabbed at her eyes.

"Well, honestly, I'm with Ned," Atlas said. "That was really anticlimactic."

I rolled my eyes. "You didn't have to come. I told you both it was no big deal."

"There is no way they were going to miss this," Ramona assured me. "We're all really happy for you, girl."

I hugged her. "Thanks. I miss the others. Video chat just isn't the same as having them here, but I understand they have to find where they belong now too. There is no doubt in my mind that this is exactly where I'm supposed to be. Oh, and did you guys see the news today?"

"No, we were heading here."

"They got him."

"Who?"

"Luther, our Collector."

"Westin Force got him?"

"Nope, he's been officially committed to a long-term mental facility. Court ordered. And his nephew took control of his estate, his company, his finances, and his assets."

"He can't come back here?"

"Nope. We're safe at last."

The four of us hugged.

"Mirage, congratulations," I heard before small arms wrapped around me.

"Bella! I wasn't expecting to see you."

Lisa shrugged. "She insisted when she heard the news."

"How's everything going?"

"Good. She's a great kid."

As Bella scooted off to play with the triplets, Lisa lowered her voice. "You know, she's still looking for a forever home."

"What?"

"As much as I love her, I'm a single mom and while foster care is fine. I'm not in a position to take legal custody of her. Just saying."

"Just saying what?"

"Maybe you and Colin would like to take custody of her. Adopt her. Give her the home she deserves. She adores you and it would keep her here in territory."

"Why are you telling me this now?"

She sighed. "The state came by for an inspection yesterday and her case worker mentioned that they had a possible family willing to take her. A human family."

Kelsey was right there beside me. "We're not going to let that happen, Lisa. I was a ward of the state. I will not condemn another shifter child to that if I can help it. I'll adopt her myself first."

"Kels, we talked about this."

"I'm not letting her go to the humans, Kyle."

"What are we talking about?" Colin asked.

"Bella may be getting adopted by a human couple," I said.

"What? Like hell she will. Do something, Kyle."

"I'm trying, but there was a mix up at the courthouse. Our normal Verndari contact there was out on maternity leave, and Bella got mixed in with every other kid in the system, so my hands are a bit tied, but I'm working on it."

"I just hope it's not too late," Lisa said.

"No," Colin said. "She's not leaving Westin territory."

"We've already reached out to everyone interested in adoption. No one wants an eight-year-old," Kelsey growled.

"We do," he blurted out. "We'll take her. Just tell me what needs to happen."

Kyle raised his eyebrow, and then slowly turned to me.

Colin whipped around to face me. "Shit! You absolutely get a say in this. I didn't mean it like that, it's just, it's Bella."

I started to cry. "Yes! You're sure?"

"I'm sure."

I hugged him and kissed him a dozen times.

"We're really going to do this?"

"I'd be lying if I said one month alone with you was enough, but it's Bella."

I nodded. "It's Bella."

"You've had a connection with her since the moment the two of you met. I think we have to do this."

"I'd say this just became an even bigger celebration," Kyle said.

"I don't want to get her hopes up just yet. Let's make sure it's not too late and this can really happen first."

Lisa hugged me. "You won't regret this."

"I know."

Kyle and Kelsey disappeared, but everyone else stayed for about an hour. The first of our guests had just left when he sent for me and Colin.

"Betsy's back in the office and she's going to fast track this, but without pressure and after having sat with this decision for an hour, I need to know how serious you are about suddenly becoming parents after one month of knowing each other."

"Make it happen," Colin said. "There is no way in hell we're losing touch with Bella. That little girl deserves more than the shit hand life dealt her."

I couldn't stop crying as I nodded. We had learned that during her kidnapping, her parents had tried to intervene and were murdered. It was too horrible to even think about.

"She's been through more than any child should already. She deserves a stable home with parents that love her," I said.

"We can be that for her."

"I don't exactly know what that looks like. I didn't have any role models for parenting. But I know I can love her and support her and figure the rest out along the way."

Colin grinned. "We'll figure it out, together."

"Betsy, did you hear that?"

"I did. I'm processing the paperwork now. She'll be yours within the next twenty-four hours. It's basically showing on paper that we found a distant relative to take her. That will grant immediate guardianship and halt any other adoption attempts. I'll be up in a few weeks to do a home check and start the official adoption process. It's all really just a formality. As soon as the guardianship is signed tomorrow, I'll alert Lisa and you can officially take custody of Bella."

"Tomorrow?" I gulped.

"Tomorrow."

We thanked her and I felt like I was walking in a dream cloud as we rejoined the party. Colin gave Lisa a thumbs up.

"Yes!" she yelled, but then ran over and hugged us both. "I don't know anyone better to support her than the two of you."

"You should hear from them tomorrow. We're going to bail early and start prepping a few things at home," Colin told her before we made our rounds to thank each person still there and say goodbye.

Last was Bella. She ran into my arms with the biggest hug.

"We're going to see you real soon, okay?"

"Promise?"

"I promise, sweet girl."

Colin had to practically pry her away from me. The decision was made. She was ours and I was ready to take her home.

We were both quiet on the drive home as the impact of our decision started to sink in. Long forgotten was the baked spaghetti I'd made, or the special night I was planning for the two of us. There were so many more important things floating through my head now.

"Holy shit! We're going to be parents."

\*\*\*\*\*

*Thank you for reading Probable Fear, a Westin Pack Delta novel.*

*If you're new to my PNR World, and can't wait for more, try starting at the book that began it all with Kyle & Kelsey in One True Mate.*

*Or jump right into Westin Force (Bravo team) starting with Grant & Taylor's story in Fierce Impact.*

*And be sure to keep reading for a special announcement regarding A New Prospect, book 4 in the Delta series. (hint, it's Tucker's story!)*

# Dear Reader,

Thanks for reading Probable Fear. If you enjoyed Colin & Mirage's story, please consider dropping a review. https://mybook.to/WestinForceDelta3 It helps more than you know.

For further information on my books, events, and life in general, I can be found online here:

Website: www.julietrettel.com

www.facebook.com/authorjulietrettel

www.instragram.com/julie.trettel

https://www.bookbub.com/authors/julie-trettel

http://www.goodreads.com/author/show/14703924.Julie_Trettel

http://www.amazon.com/Julie_Trettel/e/B018HS9GXS

Sign up for my Newsletter with a free Westin Pack Short Story! https://dl.bookfunnel.com/add9nm91rs

Love my books?
Join my Reader Group, Julie Trettel's Book Lover's on Facebook!
https://www.facebook.com/groups/compounderspod7

With love and thanks,
Julie Trettel

## Special Announcement

# A NEW PROSPECT

Wolves mate for life. For better or worse.

I've lived it all--the good, the bad, and the ugly.

Still, I don't back down on my commitments.

Living with Annie isn't always easy and some things need to change.

I need to change. But the damage runs deep.

Will we be able to overcome our past and start again?

*Watch Tucker's whole world change in A New Prospect coming December 21, 2023*

\*\*\*\*\*

Pre-order your copy today! *https://mybook.to/WestinForceDelta4*

## More books by Julie Trettel!

Westin Pack
One True Mate
Fighting Destiny
Forever Mine
Confusing Hearts
Can't Be Love
Under a Harvest Moon

Collier Pack
Breathe Again
Run Free
In Plain Sight
Broken Chains
Coming Home
Holiday Surprise

ARC Shifters
Pack's Promise
Winter's Promise
Midnight Promise
iPromise
New Promise
Don't Promise
Forgotten Promise
Hidden Promise
All-Star Promise

Westin Force
Fierce Impact
Rising Storm
Collision Course
Technical Threat
Final Extraction
Waging War

Six Pack Shifters
His Destined Mate
His True Mate
His Chosen Mate
His Fierce Mate
His Stubborn Mate

Westin Force Delta
High Risk
Nothing to Chance

Bonus Westin World Books
Ravenden
A Collier First Christmas
Panther's Pride: The Shifter Trials
Christmas at Kaitlyn's Place

## More books by: Jules Trettel!

Armstrong Academy
Louis and the Secrets of the Ring
Octavia and the Tiny Tornadoes
William and the Look Alike
Hannah and the Sea of Tears
Eamon and the Mysteries of Magic
May and the Strawberry Scented Catastrophe
Gil and the Hidden Tunnels
Elaina and the History of Helios
Alaric and the Shaky Start
Mack and the Disappearing Act
Halloween and the Secret's Blown
Ivan and the Masked Crusader
Dani and the Frozen Mishaps

Stones of Amaria
Legends of Sorcery
Ruins of Magic
Keeper of Light
Fall of Darkness

The Compounders Series
The Compounders: Book1
Dissension
Discontent
Sedition

# About the Author

Julie Trettel is a USA Today Bestselling Author of Paranormal Romance. She comes from a long line of story tellers. Writing has always been a stress reliever and escape for her to manage the crazy demands of juggling time and schedules between work and an active family of six. In her "free time," she enjoys traveling, reading, outdoor activities, and spending time with family and friends.

Visit

www.JulieTrettel.com

Made in the USA
Las Vegas, NV
09 November 2023

80493790R00140